laptop #4

power play

Beware of Broken Promises

by Christopher P.N. Maselli

Zonder**kidz**

*To my wonderful wife, Gena,
my greatest cheerleader and my Padmé*

Zonder**kidz**®

The children's group of Zondervan

www.zonderkidz.com

Power Play
Copyright © 2003 by Christopher P. N. Maselli

Requests for information should be addressed to:
Grand Rapids, Michigan 49530

ISBN: 0-310-70341-7

Editor: Gwen Ellis
Interior design: Beth Shagene and Todd Sprague
Art direction: Jody Langley

Printed in the United States of America

03 04 05 06 07 08 /❖DC/ 10 9 8 7 6 5 4 3 2 1

Contents

1

No Big Deal . . .
Really

Trust is easily found but not so easily kept. And once lost, it can be nearly impossible to regain. Some time ago, a scientist—an inventor—discovered this truth the hard way. He found the trust he freely gave to others was put to the test . . . and then shattered when they destroyed his life.

"'Blowing chunks' is *not* something we talk about at the breakfast table, Matt."

Thirteen-year-old Matt Calahan shrugged. "I didn't bring it up, Mom, you did."

Penny Calahan looked into the stainless steel toaster and adjusted her straight black hair. "Well, anyway, I don't think Gill has anything to be nervous about. He's very talented, and he'll do fine."

Matt nodded and took another bite of Raisin Bran. After swallowing, he said, "Actually, Gill isn't nervous about acting in his commercial. He's nervous because

he hates the cookies he's promoting. He says whenever he eats them, they make him bl—"

Matt's mother turned and peered down at him.

"Er . . . make him not feel well."

"Well, I'm sure Gill is glad he has friends like you
and Lamar and Alfonzo to help him through it. When
I was your age, I never had close friends I could trust
like you do. Wish I had."

Matt took a few more bites. "Yeah, we were
thinking about going to the youth group's winter
banquet together. It's coming up next Friday."

"You want to go to a *what?*"

Matt had tried to bring it up casually, but his
mother saw through him as if he were made of glass.
He focused on his Raisin Bran. Maybe she would
calm down if he didn't look at her. The bran flakes
slowly soaked up the milk in his spoon.

"A winter banquet," Matt repeated to his mother,
who was now slicing a grapefruit. "That's all."

Matt's father, smelling of musky cologne, entered
the room. "What's the hot topic?"

"Gill puking during his commercial," Matt said.

His mother shot him a disapproving look. "Matt
wants to go on a date," she announced.

Matt dropped his spoon into his breakfast bowl
with a clank. "It's *not* a date," he protested. "It's a
youth function."

"It's not a date, Penny," Matt's father said to his wife. Then to Matt, "What is it? Like a social event?"

Matt let out a breath of relief. Finally, someone understood. "Yes, a social event." He pulled his fingers through his black hair.

Mr. Calahan winked. He opted for a seat across from Matt, sat down, and leaned in. "Hey, if you need some social pointers, just ask your dad."

"Oh, yeah," Matt's mom said with a smile. "Your dad's the hippest guy on the construction site."

Mr. Calahan sat up straight. "Now, now. I carried my own weight in my day. I was quite a Casanova."

Penny Calahan set down her grapefruit. "*You* were a Casanova at age thirteen?"

"In my own right, yes ..."

"In your dreams, maybe."

Matt's parents chuckled. Matt figured it was an inside joke.

"Hey," Matt's dad said, "all I'm saying is that life is a book, and sometimes you need help plotting a chapter or two." Then to Matt, "You're a writer. You understand what I mean, don't you, Ace?"

Matt shrugged.

Mr. Calahan twisted his lip and tapped on the table. "Speaking of social events, I saw Lamar's mom at the mall last night." Then he punched, "With a *sharp*-looking guy."

Matt cringed. Lamar would be less than thrilled. He knew his mom had started seeing some guy, but he never wanted to talk about it. This was the first guy she'd dated since Lamar's father's death, right before Lamar was born. "Hmm," Matt mumbled.

"Well, I say good for her," Matt's mom cheered. "It's been way too long."

"Lamar's not too happy about it," Matt interjected.

A piercing ring filled the room.

Mr. Calahan reached for his belt and pulled off a cellular phone. "Sorry," he said, "I thought I had it on vibrate."

"You got a new phone?" Matt asked. He thought his dad had thrown away his cell phone for good since it interrupted their family time too much . . . but now he realized *that* may have been too much to expect.

Mr. Calahan looked at the display and answered, then turned back to Matt for a moment. "We'll talk about it later," he said as he left the kitchen.

"All I'm saying is that this guy Lamar's mom is dating may not be Mr. Perfect, but at least he's not a complete loser," said Mrs. Calahan.

"I guess," Matt concurred, stuffing a bite of soggy flakes into his mouth. Mrs. Calahan took a seat at the table and popped a bite of grapefruit into her mouth. Matt forced himself to get back to the initial subject—the banquet. "Mom, you don't have to be nervous. You can trust me. You said it yourself. Gill should be happy to have trustworthy friends."

"It's not just a matter of trust. It's a matter of responsibility, too."

"I'm responsible."

Stan Calahan returned to the kitchen, reclipping his cell phone to his leather belt. As he pulled a bagel and a cream cheese container out of the refrigerator, Mrs. Calahan asked, "Honey, who rushed the trash to the curb last Wednesday afternoon?"

"I did," he replied.

"Whose responsibility was it?"

"Mom, it's not the same," Matt protested.

"It's *exactly* the same." She held her saw-toothed grapefruit spoon in the air. "Taking out the trash is your responsibility every Tuesday and Friday night. And you know what? For the next month, I'm going to deduct ten percent from your allowance for every trash day you forget to put out the trash."

"*What?* What does this have to do with the winter banquet?"

"It has to do with responsibility. You're getting older, and I want you to learn responsibility."

"*Mom*, you can trust me."

"Who are you going with?" she asked.

"The guys," Matt quickly responded.

"But aren't you each taking someone? A girl?"

Matt leaned back and folded his arms across his chest. "Yeah, that's the way it works, Mom."

"That's a date, Matt. You're not old enough."

"It's not a date. It's a youth function. Ask Pastor Ruhlen."

"He's going to be there?"

"He's the one setting it up. It's the 2:52 Youth Group Winter Banquet."

"Oh. Well. Then I suppose . . ."

Mr. Calahan, now halfway through his bagel, asked, "So who are you going to take, Ace?"

Matt felt his heart speed up like a race car as his dad pushed on the pedal. His mind drifted to Isabel Zarza, who lived across the street, with the midnight black hair that flowed down her back like a waterfall and the voice that dripped like newly spun honey. He shrugged. "I haven't asked anyone yet."

"Well, who—"

Matt looked at his watch and shot up. "I gotta go—don't wanna be late for school!" He quickly put his dishes in the dishwasher and opened the counter under the sink. He pulled out the trash bag, exited through the garage, and dumped it in the old, tin trashcan on his way out. He made a mental note to drag it out to the curb after school. The trash truck never came until after school anyway.

Ten percent, he thought. *Man, I'm gonna go broke before the end of the week.*

The Enisburg Junior High lunchroom was a greasy, green-speckled, tile-floored spectacle that made any new student wonder what he was doing with his life. During lunchtime, it was especially lively, a growing roar of students with different views on life. Tables separated the jocks from the computer geeks and the hard-rockers from the math club. Matt and his three best friends, Lamar, Gill, and Alfonzo, sat at their own table, two spots away from the center of the room, where the theater students discussed their dramatic lives.

As usual, Matt sat beside Lamar Whitmore, the "spiritual one," as they called him because he was the most vocal about spiritual matters. Across from Lamar sat the newest member of their group, Alfonzo Zarza. Quite the athlete, he had moved in across the street from Matt and easily fit in with the others. Redheaded "Gill" Gillespie sat next to Alfonzo and opposite Matt, where he frequently told jokes the entire lunch period. But not today.

"I'm *so* nervous about my upcoming commercial!" he exclaimed for the third time.

"What's to be nervous about?" Lamar asked. "You know you're going to do great and become famous. At least that's what you keep telling us."

"You know *exactly* why I'm so nervous," Gill shot back. "And it's not just because the ad manager has such crazy ideas."

"What is it then?" Alfonzo questioned, egging him on, as though he didn't know.

"It's that the commercial is for Pooka Dookas!" Gill nearly shouted. "And I *hate* those cookies!"

Matt sympathized with Gill. The animal-shaped cookies with bright green jelly stuffed inside were downright ill tasting.

Gill continued his rant. "Do I have to remind you about how we always say 'Pooka Dookas make-a you puke-a!'? Only for me, it's *true!*" Gill turned to Matt. "Do you know when I was five—"

Matt buried his head in his hands and moaned. "Not this story again!"

"—I ate so many that I got sick while eating them! Green stuff went everywhere!"

Lamar threw down his sandwich. "We're eating!"

"Well, I did! And to this day, I can't stomach them! So what happens when it's time to film my commercial?" He turned to Matt again and lowered his voice. "Matt, you've gotta help me with the laptop."

The laptop. Not long ago, Matt had received this dream gift for his thirteenth birthday. It was sleek, too. As a writer, Matt loved it because now he could write anytime, anywhere. But then he discovered something exciting ... and dangerous. When he pushed a certain key on the keyboard—the one with the clock face on it—whatever was written on the screen would actually _happen._ From that day forward, Matt and his friends realized they had an awesome responsibility—as well as a dangerous tool—right at their fingertips.

"You know I won't let you down," Matt promised.

"Great!" Gill exclaimed. "And if there's ever anything I can do for you, just say the word."

Matt cut his eyes to Alfonzo and back. "Actually there is," he said thoughtfully.

"What? Anything."

"Well, you're pretty popular, Gill. How do you, you know, feel comfortable enough to ... ask someone to go to something with you?"

"You mean go to something like the winter banquet?"

Lamar turned sideways, with his back to Matt. "Ugh. I don't wanna talk about this. My mom's started going out with this guy and . . . ugh. I don't wanna talk about it."

"Matt, don't be nervous," Gill comforted. "We're all going. It's not like it's a big deal. It's just a youth function."

Matt stared at his friends. "So you've all asked someone?" They all looked down at their food. "C'mon! You all *are* going to ask someone, right? Because I am *not* going alone."

"You can count on us," Lamar promised, giving Matt a thumbs-up.

Gill and Alfonzo nodded their agreement.

Gill leaned forward. "Look, if you want to ask someone to the banquet, all you have to do is break the ice with a good joke."

Matt's eyebrows popped up. "A joke? Like what?"

Gill concentrated for a moment, then smiled. "Okay, so a string goes into a soda shop. He asks for a soda. The clerk grabs him by the neck and kicks him out, shouting, 'We don't serve strings here!' So the string goes back in. He says, 'All I want is a soda.' The clerk kicks him out again, shouting, 'I told ya, we don't serve strings here!' So the string, clearly upset, twists himself into a loop and then ruffles up his hair. He walks back into the soda shop and asks for the soda again. The clerk takes a long look at him and says, 'Hey, aren't you a string?' and the string replies, 'No, I'm a frayed knot.'" He burst into laughter at that.

Matt looked at Alfonzo, who just shrugged. Lamar rubbed his temples.

"Get it?" Gill asked. "'A frayed knot?'"

"We get it," Lamar said flatly. "We get it." He turned to Matt. "Just be who you are, Matt."

"Who am I? You mean a writer? What does a writer do? Quote Shakespeare?"

"_Great idea!_" Gill said enthusiastically. "Girls _love_ Shakespeare!"

Alfonzo shook his head. "I know just what you need to calm down, Gill."

"What?"

"I'll be right back." He squeezed out of his seat.

Matt slid out of his seat and walked beside Alfonzo.

"Hey, Alfonzo, you have any advice about asking someone out?" Matt hesitated to ask, but Alfonzo _was_ Isabel's brother. He might have an insight Matt hadn't considered.

"I'm no expert," Alfonzo returned.

"I know ... but what would you do if you were me?"

"Well, first I'd do like Lamar said. Be yourself."

"But I get all tongue-tied, my hands sweat, and I get sick to my stomach."

Alfonzo raised an eyebrow and didn't miss a beat. "Then if I were you, I'd use the laptop."

Matt looked at Alfonzo dubiously. "Really? But you know I don't like using the laptop for myself. Not for something like this."

"What could it hurt? Give yourself an edge, you know?"

The boys reached the lunchroom vending machine.

"Are you sure?" Matt asked as Alfonzo slipped fifty cents into the machine and pushed C16. Inside, a lever released, and a bag of Pooka Dookas dropped down like a can of soda.

"That's just what I'd do," Alfonzo said. "So who are you asking anyway?"

Matt looked at Alfonzo for a long moment and then shrugged.

The boys returned to their friends, and Alfonzo tossed the bag of Pooka Dookas into the center of the lunch table. Gill stared at them, looking as hopeless as a mouse in a snake cage.

"Try it," Alfonzo coaxed Gill. "You said you haven't eaten one since you were five. Maybe it's not as bad as you remember."

"It *is* as bad as I remember," Gill protested. "Besides, Matt's going to help me with the laptop!"

"Actually, Alfonzo has a point," Matt said. "Maybe you don't need the laptop. It would sure make things easier if you can just swallow one. C'mon, give it a shot."

Gill stared at the bag for another thirty seconds, and then in a swift motion, he reached out, tore it open, and shoved a Pooka Dooka in his mouth. But he didn't chew. He just sat there, face soured, staring straight ahead.

"What's up with pucker face?" demanded a loud, deep voice.

Matt turned around to see Hulk Hooligan, the school's biggest and meanest bully, standing behind him. Matt rolled his eyes.

"Nothing," Lamar responded.

Hulk nodded. "Yeah, I guess he always looks kinda like dat." Then to Lamar, "Hey, just wanted ya to know, I'm still comin' up with a way to repay ya."

Lamar waved his hands. "Please don't." Just a few weeks ago, Lamar had rescued Hulk from an exploding cabin—and ever since then, the big lug was determined to find a worthy way to pay Lamar back.

"No, I'm gonna repay ya. How 'bout I buy ya lunch? Buncha guys around here would love to gimme deir lunch money."

"No, really," Lamar insisted. "I already ate."

"Or I could show ya how to start a car without da keys. Would ya like dat?"

> **Alfonzo tossed the bag of Pooka Dookas into the center of the lunch table.**

Lamar grimaced. "No . . . thanks for the offer, though. Really, you don't have to—"

"I got it! I could—" Suddenly Hulk's head snapped back as an airborne projectile smacked him right in the face. "Aaaaaaaaaauuuuuuuuuugggghhhh!" he cried, stumbling back and nearly crushing a student on another bench.

Matt's eyes opened wide as he spun to Gill, whose mouth was empty and gaping.

Hulk stood up and stomped the floor like King Kong on a bad-hair day. The lunchroom table quaked. As he wiped his face, green goo and vanilla cookie spread to his hand.

"I couldn't hold it in anymore!" Gill shouted. "It was too gross! It just came out!"

Then it started.

The laughter.

It started with a guffaw from a drama student. And soon the entire lunchroom was belly laughing at Hulk, standing there with soggy, gooey, green gunk on his face.

Gill started shaking as Hulk balled up his mammoth fist.

"It was an accident!" Gill insisted.

"Dat was no accident!" Hulk fired back.

"It was! I couldn't hold it in!"

Hulk stepped forward, leaning over Matt, who was sure he'd just seen Gill for the last time. Then

Hulk froze. Across the room, Vice Principal Carter exited his office and stood still as a statue, his hands on his hips, staring at Hulk.

Hulk seemed to rethink his actions. He pointed a meaty finger at Gill. "Gillespie, you're gonna pay for dis. Your face is mush."

"No!" Gill pleaded. "I have to be perfect for my commercial!"

"Well, you'd better watch yer back, 'cuz before yer commercial, I'm breakin' yer nose—and _you'll_ become da laughin' stock."

And King Hulk stomped off, shaking tables in his wake.

Alfonzo let out a slight chuckle, and Gill looked at him wide-eyed. "It's not funny! He's going to kill me!"

"Been there, done that," Matt said.

"Matt, you've got to help me!" Gill cried.

Matt shook his head. "Don't worry. We'll take care of it. We'll think of something. I promise."

Casanova Calahan

2

On his way home, Matt played the scene in his mind a hundred times, but it never worked out quite right. The more he thought about asking Isabel to join him at the winter banquet, the queasier his stomach felt. Maybe, he thought, this wasn't such a good idea. But, then again, that's what an amazing laptop was for.

Matt pulled the Post-It from his mother off the front door and stuffed it in his pocket. She would be home late again tonight—another real estate appointment. And, of course, his father wouldn't be home before six. So Matt retrieved the house key from the drainpipe and let himself inside.

Before long, he was sitting at his pinewood desk in his bedroom, waiting for his laptop to boot. It was too cold outside to open the window overlooking Oleander Street, or the one by his bed. So Matt just imagined a light breeze flowing in as he looked at Alfonzo's and Isabel's house across the street. It wasn't that long ago that he had sat in the same place he was now, discovering his laptop for the first time. Only then, he had no idea about its capabilities. If he had, he wouldn't have been so careless as to write a gangster story about the old mansion and Alfonzo and Isabel moving into it. Then again ... if he hadn't, he'd have never discovered the friend he had in Alfonzo. And he'd have never met Isabel.

Matt let a long sigh escape from his lips. With the word processor open, he set his fingers on the home row of the keyboard. He knew when he met with Isabel, he had to present himself well. He knew he had to be cool ... very cool. Matt typed:

```
He wasn't just any guy. He was cool, calm,
and collected. Suave, savvy, and a general
all-around great chap. He was a man's man.
A guy's guy. Sensitive yet strong.
Compassionate yet firm. He was bold
```

Matt paused for a moment, then added:

```
and he had great hair.
```

Oh, yeah.

```
If he were a Smurf, they'd call him
Handsome Smurf. If he were a pirate,
```

> they'd call him Buccaneer Charming. If he
> were a Klingon, they'd call him ARRR. He
> was Matt Calahan, esquire, writer, talent
> extraordinaire.

A smile crept onto Matt's face. He leaned back. How could anyone turn that down? He hit the key on the Wordtronix laptop's keyboard that had a small clock face on it. He watched the on-screen cursor switch to a golden clock, the hands ticking forward like lightning. Then it turned back to the standard arrow. That's all it took, and the laptop went to work.

Matt thought about Lamar's, Gill's, and Alfonzo's advice. He sat up straight again and continued typing.

> He can quote Shakespeare like a true
> English bard. He can make 'em laugh like
> he was Jim Carrey's mentor. This is Matt,
> being himself.

Matt hit the clock key again and watched the laptop go to work. He twisted his lip. *There has to be more,* he thought. *Something I'm missing here.* He didn't want to leave any holes—any chances for something to go wrong. Matt placed his hands on the home row again.

Ka-boom-boom!

Matt jumped. His head snapped up and he peered out his bedroom window. There it was. Coming down the street. Coming fast. The dump truck.

And the garbage can was still in the garage.

Matt spun in his chair and leaped up at the same time. The chair and Matt crashed to the ground. Matt pushed himself up, then stumbled across his room and out the door. He jumped down the stairs, three at a time, and hurdled the last five at once.

Swooooosh! In his white socks, Matt slid through the kitchen, stopping at the door to the garage. He swung the door open, hit the button, and grabbed the tin trashcan as the garage door crawled upward.

Ka-boom-boom!

Matt could hear the truck drawing closer. With the garage door halfway up, Matt limboed under it, dragging the trashcan after him. The cold air hit him as he waddled down the driveway like a penguin, pulling his filthy treasure behind him. Just as the truck reached his house, the trashcan reached the curb. Matt yanked the lid off, sweating like a pig, and allowed the trash man to dump it into his truck. The man nodded to Matt and handed the container back to him. The truck rumbled down the street. Matt slammed the lid on the can and reclined on the edge, releasing a breath of relief. His mom wasn't getting 10 percent this time. He shut his eyes and suddenly had the feeling he was being watched.

Matt's eyes popped open, and there she was, standing across the street at her mailbox. Isabel. Her long, straight, midnight black hair that usually tumbled down her back like a waterfall was propped up in a floppy ponytail, sticking out from the side of her head. She wore gray sweatpants and a matching sweatshirt with clear, colored beads on it in a circular pattern. One hand hung at her side, holding her mail, and the other was raised in the air. Waving. At Matt.

Matt felt his heart pick up its pace. Though, oddly, his mouth wasn't drying up as usual. He looked down at his hands. They weren't shaking. He grinned. The laptop was doing its work. Matt lifted his right hand and waved back suavely. He took a deep breath. Feeling bold, he started across the street. Time for Buccaneer Charming to make his move.

HONK!

Matt jumped back as the oncoming car screeched to a halt.

"Sorry!" Matt apologized to the driver. The woman behind the wheel frowned at Matt and shook her head as she continued on her way. *Smooth, Matt, very smooth.*

Stupid Smurf tried again, this time looking both ways before crossing the street. When he made it across, Isabel looked slightly amused; her deep brown eyes twinkled like stars.

"You all right?" she asked.

"Yeah, I, uh, meant to do that."

She giggled.

Matt swallowed hard and said the first thing that came to mind. "Um . . . friends! Romans! Countrymen! . . . Isabel! . . . Lend me your ears!"

Isabel smirked. "Huh?"

"O Isabel, Isabel! Wherefore art thou, Isabel?"

"Oh, um, Oleander Street? Is that what you mean?"

Matt thought for a second. "To mean it or not to mean it. That is the question."

"Uh-huh."

Isabel gazed down the block. He was losing her. Matt grabbed her arm. "My words fly up, my thoughts remain below: Words without thoughts never to heaven go."

She pulled away from him. "Okay, you're freaking me out."

"Et tu, Brute?"

"I think I'd better go." She turned to leave.

"Wait!" Matt insisted. "I've got a joke."

She turned back around and looked at him.

Matt paused, "Okay. You're gonna love this. Okay. So there's this string. And he's afraid to go into a shop. 'Cuz he wants soda. So he goes in and . . . no wait . . . yeah, yeah, he goes in and says, 'Clerk, I want a soda.' The clerk says, 'We don't serve knots here,' and kicks him out. So he ruffles his hair and goes back in and asks for a soda again. And the clerk says, 'Aren't you the knot who just came in?' And he says—ready for this?—he says, 'No, I'm a frayed knot.'"

Matt laughed.

Isabel gave him a very evident courtesy laugh.

 Matt looked down. He felt a wave of embarrassment wash over him. "Okay, I'd better go," he said. "My feet are getting cold."

Isabel nodded. "Okay. See ya."

Matt looked both ways and started across the street. *How could I be so stupid? Shakespeare? Telling one of Gill's jokes! What was I thinking? Now she'll never go to the banquet with me.* Matt shook his head. *As if I'll ever get a second chance...*

"Matt?"

Matt quickly spun around when he heard her voice again, dripping like newly spun honey.

He looked at her expectantly.

"We got one of your letters again by accident." She held it out for him.

Matt returned to her side of the street. He reached out and put his fingers on the envelope but didn't take it from her. With them both holding one side, he sucked in his gut.

"Um, I'm sorry for being stupid. I, um . . . what I was trying to say is . . . um. . . . They announced a winter banquet in youth group a few weeks ago and said we could take anyone we wanted. And the guys have all had a hard time figuring out who to ask, but, um, for me, you were the first one I thought of. And if you don't want to go with me, I totally understand. No big deal. I just wanted to ask."

Isabel smiled, her eyes narrowing. "So . . . you're asking me out on a date?"

"It's really more of a youth function."

"I'd love to go."

Matt nodded. "I understand. We're all busy right now and—"

"I said yes."

Matt blinked. "You did? I mean . . . you did! Great! Great . . ." He snatched the letter from Isabel's hand and tapped it on his free hand. "I'll, um, get you all the details right away then. It'll be fun."

Isabel's eyes were twinkling again. "Okay."

He tried to keep from bursting into a goofy smile. "Okay, then. See you later."

Isabel nodded.

Matt turned on his heels and started across the street once more. He looked down at the envelope in his hand. It was addressed to him, and there was no return address. The postmark was from in town. He ripped the letter open. Inside he found a simple, white index card with a web address typed on it:

www.civd.org/messageformatt

His dark eyebrows came together as he wondered what it meant. Then a shout erupted behind him.

"Good night! Parting is such sweet sorrow!"

Puzzled, Matt stopped and looked back at Isabel.

"Shakespeare," she explained with a wink. Then she turned and ran into her house.

Matt stood there in the middle of the street, in his white socks, the cold air wrapping around him like an icy blanket. But he didn't seem to notice much, for as far as he was concerned, the sun had come out.

Matt went from absolute elation from his talk with Isabel to downright terror after he typed the mysterious address into his web browser. Right before dinner, he had looked up the website—and instantly lost his appetite. And then it didn't help that all *through* dinner, his dad kept trying to justify his new phone.

"I need a cell phone for my business," he had said.

Matt had looked up at his dad dubiously.

"But I'm approaching it differently this time," he promised. "I'm taking control of my business, Matt. I'm not letting it take control of me. My family comes first. Period. You can trust me. Just like I know I can trust you to not let your writing in your laptop control your life."

Matt just nodded. His dad had no idea what he was really facing with the laptop. He didn't know what it did. And he didn't know that when Matt first received the laptop, he ran an Internet search for Wordtronix and found a warning—a pointed warning that read:

> If you've come here, then I must be dead and you must have the Wordtronix. I hope they don't find you. I've evaded them for several years now, but I know each day their search intensifies. They want their laptop back, whatever the cost. Don't be fooled. Their promises mean nothing.
> Trust me, I know. You have power in your hands.
> Wield it well . . . as long as you can.

The warning was something Matt and his friends couldn't forget; it was always at the forefront of their minds. Because of the warning, they vowed to tell *no one* about the laptop. It was too dangerous. But the boys were smart. They traced the message back and found it was written by someone named Sam Dunaway, who lived in Landes, Arizona. When they went to his house, they found it abandoned as they expected, but they also found a secret entrance that led them to a mysterious lab, holding answers that only led to more questions. The scary part was that someone had followed them—someone in cowboy boots—someone they finally evaded. But they still wondered who it was, and if it was the same person who found Sam and the laptop ... and took Sam out of the picture.

Now, back in his room after dinner, Matt put his conversation with his dad out of his mind and shivered. He once again looked up the website printed on the index card and found himself staring at a warning. *Another* warning that read:

> **This isn't a game. The Wordtronix is not a toy.**
> **Keep using it like a toy and they WILL find you.**
> **They don't stop. They don't let up. They don't tell the truth.**
> **If things seem bad now, you'll see—it can get much worse.**
> **Much, much worse.**
>
> **If I can, I'll contact you again in a more personal way.**
> **Remember, you have power in your hands.**
> **Be smart, or any day could be your last.**

Worse! Matt wondered. *How can things get any worse! Contact me in a more personal way! What's worse than that!* Knowing there was an enemy out there was bad enough. But this was something more. Someone was *contacting* Matt. Someone knew where Matt *lived*. Someone *knew* Matt had the laptop. Matt had to get the guys together to see this message, so they could decide what to do. And soon. Very, very soon. Before someone tried to contact him in a more personal—

Bam! Bam! Bam!

The banging came from the window by Matt's bed. He slammed his laptop shut and jumped up, catching his leg in his chair. He fell to the side and then sighed with relief. It was Alfonzo. *Thank God.*

He jumped up and unlatched the window, allowing his friend inside. "Hey," Matt greeted.

"Why's your window locked?" Alfonzo said edgily.

"Something's come up. We have to meet tomorrow."

"Yeah, something's come up all right," Alfonzo shot back sharply.

"You all right?"

"You asked Iz out on a date."

"It's not a date. It's—"

"It's asking my *sister* out. When you asked for advice, you were asking about my *sister?*"

"Well, I—"

"Did you use the laptop?"

"Well, you said I could give myself an edge—"

"Not with Iz!" Alfonzo stepped forward and pushed Matt's shoulder.

> **Matt recoiled in shock at psycho Alf.**

Matt recoiled in shock at psycho Alf, who was usually so quiet. Matt hadn't seen this side of him before.

"I can't believe it!" Alfonzo exclaimed, then pressed, "You used the laptop to force her to go out with you, didn't you?"

"Wait—you don't think she'd go out with me on her own?"

"I don't care if she would or not. You can't use the laptop on her! This is my sister we're talking about."

"But it was *your* advice!"

"I didn't know you were talking about my *sister!*" Alfonzo's eyes beamed at Matt.

Matt lowered his voice and tried a different approach. "Look, I know it's your sister. I'm sorry I didn't tell you. But trust me, I didn't *force* her into anything."

Alfonzo kept his gaze on Matt.

"The truth is, the laptop didn't help at all. And neither did quoting Shakespeare. I mean it. Isabel going out with me has nothing to do with the laptop. You can trust me with this."

Alfonzo stayed quiet.

"C'mon. *Trust.* That's what the four of us—the QoolQuad—are all about, right? Think about it: Has there ever been a time I've lied to you?"

Alfonzo was still quiet.

"Ever?"

"I guess not."

"Then I'm not going to lie to you now. You can trust me with Isabel." Then Matt added, "But what's the big deal anyway? It's not like it's *Hulk* taking her out. It's *me*."

Alfonzo looked out the window, at his house across the street. "The big deal is that she's had her heart broken already when Mama left. She doesn't need that again."

"Whoa—Alfonzo. I'm taking her to the winter banquet. It's not like it's a commitment or anything. It's simply a fun dinner out."

"Fine. Just give me your word that you won't use the laptop on her."

Matt paused. "Yeah, of course."

Alfonzo let out a long breath and sat on Matt's bed, relieving the tension. "Okay. Fine. She just doesn't need any trouble in her life. And being your friend means being in trouble sometimes because you have that laptop. I don't want her in on this."

"Hey, I'm in complete agreement. No one can know about this. It's too dangerous."

"I'm serious, Matt. She doesn't need trouble of any kind."

"It's just a youth function."

"Well . . . be prepared in case she's thinking it's more than that."

"She's twelve. I'm thirteen. It can't *be* more than that. I don't *want* it to be more than that. How'd you find out, anyway?"

"Iz asked me if I knew what color you were going to wear."

Matt's forehead wrinkled, and he deflated into his desk chair. "Color? What does she mean?"

"I have no idea."

"Well, tell her green, because I'm going to be sick," Matt said, his voice trailing off.

"What?"

"Forget it."

"You say green? What color green?"

"Green is green."

"Well, there's like forest green, Kermit green, pea green, all kinds of green. She's going to ask."

"Forest green?"

Alfonzo nodded.

Matt looked at Alfonzo for a long moment, then back to his laptop, sitting quietly on his pinewood desk. He put his hands over his face and closed his eyes tight. This was more than he had asked for. No question about it: He was in *way* over his head.

3

Dropping Like Flies

Dude!" Mick Ruhlen, Matt's youth pastor, shouted. "Glad you could make it!" A lanky fellow with an eccentric personality, Pastor Ruhlen was born to be a youth pastor. The more Matt attended youth group, the more he respected the man, despite the fact that his Chia-pet hair was a different color every time Matt saw him. Today it was green. *Stoplight* green, if Matt had to narrow it down.

"Thanks," Matt said, then nodded to Lamar and Alfonzo, who'd arrived before him. Two weeks prior, they had promised Pastor Ruhlen they would help plan for the banquet. So now, on this Saturday afternoon, the three boys were here to help in any way they could. "Where's Gill?"

"He's coming," Lamar assured. "He has his commercial practice after this, so he's getting all—"

"Spiffied up," Pastor Ruhlen put a box on a table.

"Yeah. He should be here soon."

Pastor Ruhlen pulled out a measuring tape and tossed it to Matt.

"This is it, guys," Ruhlen said. "When this banquet is over, it's all downhill to the new year."

"No more work, eh?" Lamar asked.

Pastor Ruhlen shrugged. "Well, I still have to create a float for the annual parade, but that's easer-oni after this." He winked. "Hey, you guys wanna be on the float?"

"No!" Matt, Lamar, and Alfonzo all said at the same time.

"You sure? I was thinkin' of doin' this great surfin' theme and—"

Suddenly the room fell silent. Everyone spied Hulk Hooligan standing at the entrance. "My dad said I had to help."

Matt glanced at Lamar and Alfonzo. They were thinking the same thing: *Gill is going to faint when he sees Hulk is here!*

"Right on!" Pastor Ruhlen exclaimed as he approached Hulk and handed him a pad of yellow paper and a pencil. "Your job is to count ceiling tiles. I wanna hang a snowflake from each one."

"I hafta count ceiling tiles?"

"It's a dirty job, but someone hasta do it," Pastor Ruhlen said in his Clint Eastwood voice. He handed a pad of white paper to Lamar and a few pairs of scissors to Alfonzo. "You guys are the official snowflake cutters. Cut as many as Hulk says ya need."

Alfonzo said, "Great . . ."

"Matt, let's you and I measure the distance from the door to each table. Then we can cut out paper snow walkways. And we'll be walkin' in a winter wonderland!"

"In California?" Matt questioned.

"No better place!"

Hulk stopped counting. "Ya made me lose count. I was already over ten."

"Sorry," Pastor Ruhlen apologized. Then, "So, y'all have companions ta join ya?"

"My parents aren't sold on me bringing a date," Matt said flatly.

"Well, it's not a date, Matt my boy, it's a youth function. I want y'all to come with a young lady so you can get comfortable treating them with integrity and honor."

"I guess."

Pastor Ruhlen grabbed the end of Matt's tape from the tape measure and walked ten paces. He read the number and then let it snap back. "Oh, yeah. Living in integrity and honor and treating others right is all part of being a member o' the 2:52 youth group. You know what Luke 2:52 says, don't ya?"

At the same time, Matt, Lamar, Alfonzo, and Hulk all said, "'Jesus grew in wisdom and stature, and in favor with God and men.'"

"Right-e-o! He grew smarter, stronger, deeper, and cooler. And just like him, you guys are doing that—and this is all part of the growing process. Gotta learn to treat women right."

"I guess," Matt said again.

A few measurements later and Gill popped into the room—"Hi guys, I'm"—saw Hulk—"outta here!"—and left.

"Gill!" Pastor Ruhlen shouted. "Gill Gillespie! Boy, come back here!"

Gill peeked his red head around the corner.

"Yah," the youth pastor said, "ya found the right place. C'mon in and give us a hand!"

Gill looked at Hulk, who growled, put down his paper and pencil, and threw his fist into his hand. Gill covered his nose. "I don't think I can stay," he whimpered, never taking his eyes off Hulk.

Pastor Ruhlen looked at Hulk and back at Gill. "Nonsense," he said. "Don't let the big guy scare ya. He's just a big teddy bear, ain't ya, Hulk?"

Hulk growled again. Gill chuckled nervously and stepped into the room. He slid along the wall, past Hulk, keeping his distance. Matt didn't know what he was so worried about. It wasn't like Hulk would do anything to him with Pastor Ruhlen standing there.

"Why're ya so nervous?" Hulk asked, daring him to say something . . . *anything.*

Gill let Hulk off the hook. "I'm nervous because the ad manager for my commercial is getting weirder ideas every time I show up to a practice."

Hulk rolled his eyes and went back to counting.

"How bad can it be?" Lamar wondered.

"He wants to put me in a polka outfit."

Lamar stopped cutting his snowflake. "Okay, that's bad. Are they going to make you actually *dance* the polka?"

Hulk snickered, then frowned, obviously losing count again.

"I don't know. I don't care. It doesn't matter. I still can't get myself to swallow a Pooka Dooka anyway."

Matt quipped, "So your problem is the perilous possibility of puking Pookas while performing polkas?"

Gill nodded. "Precisely. It's the price I pay."

"For what?"

"Popularity."

Gill grabbed a sheet of paper and a pair of scissors and started cutting. "Oh, by the way," he said, "speaking of my crazy ad manager, he changed the date of the commercial. Now we're doing it live at the next HockPucks hockey game. They're playing a team from Michigan, and attendance is supposed to be high. He says it's the kind of big, affordable TV event he's looking for to debut the new ad campaign."

Alfonzo's eyes grew wide. "The HockPucks? Now *there* are some guys who know their stuff! Can we watch the game from behind the players' bench?"

"Sure," Gill said.

"Can we meet the players?"

"Sure."

"Can we play hockey with them?"

"Don't push it."

"This is *sooo* cool," Lamar said. "I can't wait. Thanks, Gill."

"Four feet," Matt read from the measuring tape to Pastor Ruhlen. Then he stopped cold. "Wait a second. When is your commercial again?"

"During the next HockPucks game."

"Right. And when is *that?*"

"Next Friday night."

"Gill, that's the same night as this banquet." Pastor Ruhlen looked up at the boys.

"It is?"

"Yeah."

"I guess I can't make the banquet then. I'm under contract."

Matt looked at Gill for a long moment. Sure, Gill didn't have much of a choice, but they had agreed to go to the banquet together.

"Pastor Ruhlen, you'll understand if we can't make it, won't you?" Alfonzo asked.

"If *we* can't make it?" Matt interrupted. "What do you mean *we?* The rest of us *can* make it."

"Not me," Alfonzo said matter-of-factly. "I'm

watching the HockPucks game from behind the players' bench."

Matt just stared at Alfonzo dumbfounded. They had all agreed to go to the banquet *together*. Matt risked everything asking Isabel to join him, and now his friends were dropping like flies. Matt looked at Lamar.

"Hey, I'm still with you," Lamar assured Matt. "Unless I can't find anyone to take."

"Then what? You're out, too?"

Lamar shrugged.

"I thought we were in this together," Matt said softly. He looked at Hulk.

"I ain't goin' to no stupid girly winter banquet," he announced. Then his eyes narrowed. "But . . ." His gaze shifted to Lamar. "Ya know . . ."

Lamar asked, "Why are you looking at me like that?"

"Yeah . . ."

"Yeah, what?"

"Yer goin' to the banquet *for sure*."

"How's that?"

"I got a way to pay ya back. Yer goin' with my cousin."

"I'm what?"

"Yer goin' to the banquet with my cousin."

"Thank you!" Matt exclaimed.

"Matt!" Lamar scolded.

"What?" Hulk demanded, clenching his fists. "Ya don't wanna go out with Nick?"

"A guy?"

"Nicki," Hulk corrected. "She's cool, and she needs someone safe now dat she's outta JD."

"Juvenile Detention?" Lamar exclaimed. "What was she in for?"

Hulk cracked his knuckles. "Dat's in the past. It's my way of payin' ya back. Dank ya very much."

"But—"

"End of talk!" And Hulk exited the room.

"I guess you're going out with Nick," Alfonzo said to Lamar.

"Nicki," Lamar corrected. "And no, I'm not. You have to go talk him out of it."

"Why me?" Alfonzo asked.

"It's the least you can do," Matt said sorely, "after breaking your promise about the banquet."

"But, Gill—"Alfonzo shook his head. "Fine."

Gill jumped in, "Ooo! And talk him out of breaking my nose, *please!*"

"Whatever." And Alfonzo exited the room.

Matt huffed. "You still have to find someone to go with, Lamar. I'm not going alone."

"I'll do my best," Lamar said.

"You know, my confidants," Pastor Ruhlen said suddenly, "this might be a good opportunity to put some faith in the Big Guy above. Part of growing up in God is learning to trust him, too. Putting your faith in him. Believing him for working things out when it doesn't seem we as mere men can."

Matt set his tape measure on a table. *Maybe,* he thought. *But it was more than that. It was about Gill and Alfonzo breaking their promise. It was about Matt possibly being stuck at the banquet alone—and having* no *idea what to do when he got there.*

At once, Alfonzo walked back into the room. Everyone looked at him expectantly.

"Well?" Lamar asked.

"You're not getting out of going out with Nick."

"Nick*i.*"

"Right. His heart is set on it. Says he owes you."

"What about me?" Gill asked.

"That's the good news. He agreed not to break your nose."

"Yes!"

"So long as he can watch the game from behind the players' bench, too."

"No!"

"Yes! I already told him he could. What's the problem? I've saved your nose."

"The *problem* is that now he'll be closer than ever—ready to extract revenge!" Gill suddenly gasped and lifted his hands to the sky. "I know what evil he has planned! He's gonna make his move at the game!" Gill put his hands down and grabbed Matt's arm. "You have to help me!"

Pastor Ruhlen looked at Matt. Matt widened his eyes at Gill, warning him to stay quiet about the laptop.

"I'll help you all I can," Matt said, coded, and pulled his arm away.

"But I need you *there!* How can you help me if you're at the banquet?"

"Don't even think about canceling on Iz," Alfonzo warned. Then he turned to the others. "You guys know he asked Iz to the banquet?"

Lamar and Gill nodded and shrugged as if to say, "Well, yeah, what did you expect?"

"I must be blind," Alfonzo said to no one in particular.

"I don't know what I'm going to do," Matt admitted. "I don't know why I have to keep my end of the bargain when none of you want to keep yours!"

"*I* have no choice!" Gill shouted.

"Dudes," Pastor Ruhlen addressed them, "I think y'all need to have an ultimate chill-out party. I've never seen you dudes like this."

"These guys have never broken their promises to me before," Matt shot back.

"Trust God," Pastor Ruhlen pressed. "He can help you guys through this. Meanwhile, y'all need to do something to relax."

The four boys stared at each other quietly, each with his arms folded across his chest.

Finally Matt remembered the laptop message he wanted to show his friends. Despite all this mess, he knew they would have to pull together and decide what to do about it. "Why don't you guys come over to my house after we're done here?" he suggested. "I have something to show you on my computer."

"Tomorrow night," Gill said. "I've got commercial practice after this." Then his eyes lit up. "But why don't you guys come to my practice? You can see some of the players. Maybe even talk to them."

"Talk to them?" Matt asked.

Gill nodded.

Matt's eyes darted to Lamar. Yes, they were in over their heads, but maybe some of these guys who "know their stuff"—these hockey players—could provide some desperately needed pointers. Matt smiled. Well, it wouldn't hurt to ask . . .

Slapshot Advice

4

*S*wish! *Swish! Pop!*

Like hurricanes on skates, the HockPucks shot the hockey puck around the skating rink with ease. Matt, Lamar, Gill, and Alfonzo stared in awe at the players, all geared up, zipping around the rink.

"I want to skate with them *so bad*," Alfonzo said.

"Hello, Conrad Gillespie!" The four boys turned around to see a short, fat man with flat, black hair, a thin mustache, and red suspenders. In his left hand was a hanger holding a white suit with purple polka dots. "This is for you," he said, in a slightly French accent, handing the suit to Gill.

"Hi, uh, these are my friends," Gill said, then turned to the others. "This is Carl, my ad manager for the commercial."

Matt opened his mouth to respond, but Carl the ad manager had already grabbed Gill's arm and started to walk. "I've made a few changes," he said as they moved away.

Lamar lifted his eyebrows. "They're going to make him wear a polka-dot suit?"

"Makes *me* wanna eat Pooka Dookas," Matt said.
Lamar rolled his eyes. "Seriously."

Matt, Lamar, and Alfonzo walked around the rink, watching the players through tall Plexiglas dividers. It seemed strange to see the arena so empty. The only other time Matt had been in the building thousands of fans were screaming their heads off. Now there were just silent, hanging advertisements, a darkened scoreboard, and echoes of sticks and pucks cracking against the ice.

The players on the ice were geared up, with generous layers of padding on their elbows and knees. Most of them were just knocking the puck around the neutral zone. In both defensive zones, around the crease, a player or two was trying to get a line of pucks past a goalie.

At a nearby opening, Alfonzo pointed to number 46, a player shooting pucks into the goal.

"Check it out," Alfonzo said. "That's Hot Shot Howard. Season's only half over and he's had two hat tricks already. Watch him—he won't miss one."

Pop! Pop! Pop! Pop! Pop! Alfonzo was right. One after another, Hot Shot lifted them into the net with precision. The last one slid right between the goalie's legs. The goalie seemed completely baffled. When Hot Shot finished his row of pucks, he spotted the boys watching him. Alfonzo waved. Hot Shot skated over and swished to a stop right in front of them.

"You're Hot Shot Howard!" Alfonzo shouted.

"Howard's fine," he said, his voice deep. "Nice to meet ya."

"Can you teach me how to shoot like that?" Alfonzo begged.

Howard laughed. "Years of practice. But you want to see a *real* trick?"

Alfonzo was all ears.

Howard exited the ice and took a seat on a nearby bench. "Watching?"

Alfonzo nodded. Matt looked at Lamar, who shrugged.

> **Hot Shot skated over and swished to a stop right in front of them.**

"Say, 'go,'" Howard ordered.

"Go!"

At once, Howard threw off his gloves and ran his hands over his skate laces like lightning. Seconds later, both skates lay on the floor.

Alfonzo's mouth dropped. "You did that in like . . . ten seconds."

Howard bobbed his eyebrows up and down. "Say 'go' again."

"Go!"

Ten seconds later, the skates were back on Howard's feet.

"You *gotta* teach me how to do that," Alfonzo begged, his mouth watering.

Hot Shot Howard patted the bench. "Have a seat, I'll show ya the trick."

Lamar headed toward the seat, too, but Matt stopped him with a slap on his chest. He nodded toward the center of the ice rink. The ad manager had cleared the hockey players out of the neutral zone . . . and now Gill stood in the face-off circle at center ice . . . all duded up in his white and purple polka-dot suit, with a bag of Pooka Dookas in his hand.

Matt and Lamar moved up to the boards to watch.

Gill carefully stepped back several paces. Matt watched as Carl the ad manager pressed a button on a boom box in front of him. Suddenly, out of the little speakers, some *big* polka music started playing.

Boo-buhda-boo-boo! Boo-buhda-boo-boo!

Carl motioned to Gill. Like a chicken, Gill strutted forward, doing his own version of the polka that was sure to get a barrel of hockey-fan laughs. He slid to the center of the rink.

Boo-buhda-boo-boo! Boo-buhda-boo-boo!

"Look this way!" the ad manager shouted. "The camera will be straight ahead!"

As the music faded, Gill put on a big smile. He lifted up the bag of Pooka Dookas and showed it to the imaginary camera.

He shouted, "Kids! Looking for something sweet and crunchy? Pooka Dookas!"

Carl the ad manager smiled big and waved his hands. "You don't have to yell, Conrad. You'll have a microphone clipped to you."

"Oh, sorry."

"Continue. And keep dancing. It adds a little flair."

Matt and Lamar found it hard suppressing their laughs. The hockey players, watching from around the rink, didn't bother suppressing theirs.

Gill continued, "Kids! Looking for something sweet and crunchy? Pooka Dookas!" He pulled one out of the bag. "Parents! Looking for something with a nutritious surprise inside? Pooka Dookas!" He started dancing more. "Looking for something that will put a spring in your step? A jolt in your jog? A kick in your dance?"

"You bet I am!" Matt exclaimed to Lamar, who was covering his face and laughing.

"Then get Pooka Dookas—now in three new colors, including polka dots!"

"You've got to be kidding!" Lamar said.

"Just one taste and you'll say"—Gill pretended to toss a Pooka Dooka in his mouth—"Pooka Dookas are supa-dupa!"

Matt added, "And they make-a you puke-a!"

Carl the ad manager clapped his hands and then studied his clipboard. "Okay, good. Let's try it again from the top, and this time, we'll work on your placement on the ice."

Matt and Lamar shook their heads. "Too much," Lamar said, wiping his eyes. "Too much." Then to Matt, "Now what?"

"Well, you know, I was thinking. My dad says life is like a book and sometimes you need help plotting the next chapter. Since we're stuck going to the banquet, maybe these guys could give us some advice. Help us plot our strategy. Alfonzo said they know their stuff, right?"

"Yeah, about hockey, but . . . I don't know, Matt."

Suddenly Matt felt a tap on his shoulder.

"'Scuse me," said number 24, holding his helmet in his hands. His curly blond hair clung to his forehead. "I overheard you say you're looking for advice. About hockey?"

Matt looked at Lamar. Lamar looked at Matt.

"Actually," Matt began, "we're going to this winter banquet and we're looking for advice about—"

"Ah! Dating!"

"Well, it's really more of a youth function."

Number 24 leaned into the rink. "Guys! Come over here!" he yelled to his friends.

Lamar shot a look at Matt as if to say, *What did you just get us into?*

Twenty-four boldly announced, "These guys want advice about goin' out."

Number 56 elbowed his way in front of his buddies. "Oh, well, let me tell ya . . . Here's the thing, guys," he said with a meaty finger in Matt's face. "You gotta give it your all. Ya gotta get out there, play the game, work real hard, and do your best."

Matt and Lamar just nodded.

"The competition might give it their best shot, but you have to stand strong, use your heads."

"Uh-huh," Matt said.

"You know, you work real hard, practice all you can, and then give it a hundred ten percent. No less."

Number 88 knocked 56 out of the way. "Going out with a girl is a lot like playing hockey for the first time."

"It is?" Lamar asked.

"Oh, yeah. Think about it. You're both going out, unsure, onto the slippery ice of a new relationship. So you get out there, ya skate around a little bit, knock around conversational tidbits, and try not to break the rules."

Matt asked, "Rules?"

"Rule number one: Don't lose your wits, or you'll run into the wall and everyone on the other side of the glass will laugh at you. And rule number two: If you get in a fight, be the first to back down. Just say it was your fault."

Lamar's face scrunched up. "Isn't that lying?"

"If you don't," number 88 said, "you could end up in the penalty box."

Player 63 jumped in next. He put one arm around Matt and one around Lamar. "Here's my philosophy, boys," he said in a near-whisper. "Courting is a pleasure, but parting is grief."

"How's that?" Lamar asked.

"'Cause, a false-hearted lover is worse than a thief."

"Well, thanks, guys!" Matt burst. "I think that's about everything we needed to know! We'll remember your advice," he promised, his voice trailing off, "especially if we ever get stuck on top of Old Smoky."

"What are we going to do?" Matt asked Lamar as they pulled away from the group.

"We are in so much trouble. If those guys can't get their strategy straight, what hope is there for us?"

Matt huffed. "We wouldn't be in this mess if everyone was going. It'd be easier then." Matt watched Gill practicing his commercial and Alfonzo talking to Hot Shot Howard. It wasn't supposed to be this way. They were supposed to be in this together. "It's like they're breaking up our team."

Just then, from the center of the arena, Matt heard Carl the ad manager instruct Gill, "Okay, actually *eat* the Pooka Dooka this time."

"But—"

"Don't worry. There are lots more where that came from!"

"But—"

"C'mon, c'mon! Let's go!"

Reluctantly Gill went through the whole polka routine again, but this time: "Just one taste and you'll say"—Gill actually threw a Pooka Dooka into his mouth—"Pooka Dookas are . . . are . . ." His face soured. "Are ..." He coughed and started to gag. "Supa-dupa!" Then when the ad manager looked down at his clipboard, Gill spit the chewed cookie into his hand and quickly shoved it into his pocket.

"Gross," Matt said.

"Not bad!" Carl congratulated. "You'll do great after a few more practices."

"Water!" Gill cried.

"All right, take five."

Gill slid across the rink and was soon at Matt's side, polka dots and all. "Matt, you *have* to help me out! You have to skip the banquet!"

Alfonzo caught up with the group and shot Matt a warning look.

Gill just stared at Matt, like a lost puppy.

"I'll do the best I can," Matt said truthfully.

"What does that mean?" Gill demanded.

Alfonzo answered for him. "I think you're on your own, amigo."

Calling the Whole Thing Off

5

Bam! Bam! Bam!

Matt jumped up, knocking his chair over and crashing to the ground. He peered out over the top. Lamar. He pushed himself up, walked over, and unlocked the window.

"What're you locking your window for?" Lamar asked.

"That's what we're meeting about tonight. You're early."

"*Yeah*, I'm early."

"What's that supposed to mean?"

"That's supposed to mean exactly what I said."

"So why are you early again?"

Lamar tapped his foot. He collapsed on Matt's bed. "You know that guy my mom is seeing?"

"Not personally."

"Turns out he's taking her to our winter banquet."

"Aren't they a little old to come to youth group?"

"As *chaperones*," Lamar explained.

Matt's shook his head in empathy. "Man, I'm sorry." He picked up his chair and sat down.

"I'm not crazy about this guy as it is. Now I have to sweat it out the whole night while I'm sitting with the girl from JD."

"Man, I'm *so* sorry. This just keeps getting worse. You know what Alfonzo told me?"

"That he doesn't want you to use the laptop on his sister?"

"Well, that, yes . . . but he also told me Isabel wants to know what color I'm wearing."

Lamar pursed his lips. "Why?"

"I have no idea. Maybe she's knitting me some drapes."

"We're in way over our heads, Matt. I mean in *way* over our heads."

"This would be easier if we were *all* going."

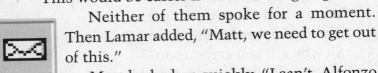Neither of them spoke for a moment. Then Lamar added, "Matt, we need to get out of this."

Matt looked up quickly. "I can't. Alfonzo wouldn't be too thrilled."

"If you go out with Isabel and mess things up, he'll be even less thrilled."

"Well, that's true. And it's not like he and Gill kept their word to us."

"That's what I'm saying."

"But Alfonzo said she's been through a lot, you know, with her parents' divorce. I don't want to bring her any more disappointment."

"Which is exactly *why* we need to cancel—before we mess up and disappoint everyone, including ourselves. We need to get out of this. Now. Before we regret our very existence."

Matt nodded. "You know, for the optimistic, encouraging guy you are, you're not doing so well."

Lamar shrugged.

"Okay, you're right. If we're going to get out of it, let's at least do it fast." Matt swung around in his desk chair and popped open his laptop. It was already booted, so he just launched the word processor. He typed:

> Matt Calahan, esquire, writer, talent extraordinaire, had made a difficult decision. It was time to tell Isabel Zarza that, for now, they were headed down two different paths . . . two different lanes on the highway of destiny.

Lamar leaned over Matt's shoulder. "Careful— you said you wouldn't use the laptop to influence Isabel."

"I'm not," Matt countered. "I'm just going to get us in the same place at the same time."

"Ah . . . so where are you going to meet her?"

Matt scratched his chin—he wasn't sure why. It was just the writer thing to do. "Has to be somewhere in public."

"Right!" Lamar agreed. "Whenever dealing with a potentially threatening situation, it's best to do it in public."

"Exactly. It'll stifle any potential outburst." Matt started to type but then stopped. It had to be somewhere that Isabel would be calm . . . somewhere *anyone* would be calm.

> Matt met Isabel at Snowy Joe's. He was waiting for her . . . and when she arrived, he had just the words to say to break it to her easily.

"Ah, an ice cream parlor," Lamar congratulated Matt. "Good idea. Who can get mad over ice cream?"

"Who, indeed."

"Okay, now me."

Matt typed:

> Lamar Whitmore, spiritual man and misunderstood artist, had a story that was quite different. Quite simply, he wasn't quite ready to go out with someone with a criminal past . . . quite criminal.

"What'd she do?" Lamar asked.

"How should I know?"

"You wrote it."

"Anyway . . ."

> He met her at Happy Gas.

"The gas station? You meet Isabel at an ice cream parlor, and I meet Hulk's cousin at a gas station?"

Matt gave Lamar a sideways glance.

Lamar shrugged. "Yeah, I guess that's about right."

Matt continued,

> He was waiting for her . . . and when she arrived, he had just the words to say to break it to her easily.

Matt hit the clock key on the keyboard. At once, the on-screen cursor flashed to a golden clock, swiftly ticking forward, and then it turned back to the boring arrow. It was final.

Lamar put his hand on Matt's shoulder. "One for all and all for one," he said. "I'm glad we're doing this together."

"One for all and all for one," Matt repeated.

"Wait," Lamar interrupted the moment. "How will I know who she is? I've never seen her before."

Matt closed his laptop. "That's easy," he said. "Just picture Hulk with a ponytail."

Matt's knee was bobbing up and down, a hundred miles an hour, as he sat in Snowy Joe's and waited for Isabel, who was up at the counter ordering ice cream. The confrontation was inevitable now; he had set it up, and she had arrived. When she first entered, she'd seen him immediately, sitting at the back of the parlor, and had waved. She then approached him on her own, gave him a "Fancy meeting you here!" and told him she'd be right back. Now she stood at the counter, waiting for Snowy Joe to finish compiling her order.

Snowy Joe, a bald, dark-skinned man in his fifties, made all the ice cream by hand. Rumor was that he had nearly a thousand ice cream recipes, though he never had more than about twenty at one time. Finally he handed Isabel her order. She grabbed two napkins and a spoon and headed toward Matt.

"Hola!" she greeted. "May I join you?"

Matt nodded nervously, wondering why he was sweating like a pig both times he had seen her this past week. Last time he was taking out the trash. This time he was *feeling* like trash. Isabel pulled a shiny, red metal chair back and sat down, placing her Styrofoam ice cream bowl on the table.

Matt had ordered "the usual"—a Choc-Choc-Choc. Isabel had ordered the Vanilla Bunny. The Choc-Choc-Choc was chocolate ice cream crammed with chocolate chips and topped with chocolate syrup. The Vanilla Bunny was vanilla ice cream mixed with coconut and marshmallows. To give it personality, Snowy Joe had put a couple chocolate-chip eyes on one side of Isabel's scoop and a mini-marshmallow tail on the opposite side. Obviously Isabel couldn't resist.

"I couldn't resist," Isabel said. "I don't know what got into me. I normally don't want ice cream on cold days like this. But today . . . I just got the urge!"

"Heh-heh," Matt said. "How about that . . ."

Matt took one last bite of his Choc-Choc-Choc and shoved the spoon into the dark brown mound of ice cream. His appetite was quickly waning.

"Want the tail?" Isabel asked, pointing to the mini-marshmallow on her scoop of ice cream.

Matt shook his head, then let out a long breath and brushed his hand through his hair.

The words were there, on the tip of his tongue, ready to leap out, but Matt knew he had to open his mouth to free them. He'd simply tell her how much he respected her, but, golly gee, it turns out Gill's commercial is on the same night as the banquet. Being a supportive friend, of course, he had to be there. Probably better anyway, because now she wouldn't have to be concerned about what to wear. Nor would she have to fret about what color Matt was wearing. Plus, she had to appreciate that Matt was supporting his friend, watching Gill's commercial with her brother. Matt was sure she'd understand, because she was rational and forgiving and probably thinking the same thing. In fact, she probably came to the ice cream parlor because she *knew* Matt would be there. She knew he was the type of guy who liked ice cream no matter what the season, and this, she knew, was the perfect opportunity to tell *him* that *she* couldn't attend because she had to do her nails. Or her hair. Or feed her hamster. Then Matt would be totally relieved, because that's all he wanted in the first place, for both of them to feel relaxed and respectful of each other's choices.

Matt and Isabel stared into their ice cream for a long moment until they looked up at the same time and said each other's name.

They both laughed nervously.

"You first," Isabel yielded.

Matt ran his tongue along the back of his teeth. He knew it. He was right. She came to get out of the banquet. Perfect! He'd seen this happen on many sitcoms. If he let her get out of it first, he wouldn't be the bad guy, so . . . "No, you first."

"No, really, go ahead."

"No," Matt insisted. "Really. You go first."

Isabel popped a spoonful of the rabbit into her mouth and then stuffed her spoon into her ice cream. She pushed it away as she swallowed.

"Um, Alfonzo told me about the hockey game."

"Yeah. And Gill's commercial."

"Yeah. But I think Alfonzo's more interested in the hockey game. Anyway, he told me he's not going to the banquet."

"Yeah, well . . . I understand. All a matter of priorities. You know, to me, the hockey game isn't really important at all."

"Oh! I know that!" Isabel exclaimed, her hand coming to rest on the table, inches away from Matt's.

"Y-you do?"

Isabel leaned in. "Matt, I just want you to know how much I respect you for not canceling when your friends did. I know it must not be easy—I mean, you guys do everything together—but it just goes to show the kind of man you are."

Matt sat stunned for a long moment, then, "Well, I'm not sure about being a man, but . . ."

"Oh, no! You are! And it means so much to me that you have kept your promise and haven't tried to get out of the banquet for a stupid game."

"*Stupid* game," Matt agreed.

"So anyway. That's it. I'm just.... I'm just really looking forward to it. I've been through a lot this past year and . . . I could use a good, fun time away from it all."

"I . . . oh, yeah, well, oh . . . yeah."

Isabel sat back. "I'm going to wear a new dress I got to go with your forest green. That's what Alfonzo said you're wearing, right?"

"I . . . certainly hope so."

"Great." Isabel pushed a wayward strand of her long, black hair behind her ear. "So. What is it you wanted to tell me?"

Matt felt his knee starting to bob up and down again. He lifted his hand from the table and held it in the air as if he was about to speak like Socrates. And he looked into her deep brown eyes. And he swallowed hard. And he realized that what he was about to say would mean he was going to the banquet alone. Well, without his friends. And somehow, he was all right with that.

"I just wanted to say . . . I'm really looking forward to it, too."

Isabel smiled wide, her teeth glistening.

Well, Matt thought, *at least now I can figure out what it feels like to mess up and regret my very existence.*

Cram Session

6

Later that day, Matt slouched on his living room couch, watching *The Phantom Menace* on video, when he heard the rapping on the front door. "Come in!" he shouted.

Lamar entered and closed the door behind him. He crashed down beside Matt and watched the pod race without saying a word. When Anakin finally won, he asked, "So . . . how'd it go?"

Matt took a deep breath. "It went all right," he said slowly.

Lamar nodded.

"Okay, I couldn't do it," Matt said, fessing up. "But don't get mad. My punishment is that I have to go alone now."

Lamar turned his head and looked at Matt. "You're not going alone."

Matt turned his head and looked at Lamar.

Lamar admitted. "I couldn't do it either. And now my punishment is that I have to spend an evening watching my mom and her date at the banquet. He's probably a serial killer."

"He's not a serial killer."

"Well, I walked into Happy Gas, looking for Hulk with a ponytail."

"And . . ."

"And I saw this girl with short, brown hair and a nose ring."

"A nose ring?"

"A nose ring."

"So you recognized her . . . from the nose ring?"

"No, what clued me in was the tattoo on her arm. It said, 'Nicki.'"

"Oh, yeah. Well, that's a pretty good clue."

"As well as a good conversation starter. I approached her, introduced myself, and was ready to tell her that I couldn't go to the banquet."

"But . . ."

"But then she looks at me with these bright blue eyes and says, 'I just wanted to say thanks.'"

"For . . ."

"For taking her to the banquet. She says she's been running with the wrong crowd and she's looking forward to getting away from everything and turning around."

"Wow."

"Yeah. Major guilt trip. She's from Kirksville, that little town about an hour from here. I didn't even know there was a wrong crowd *in* Kirksville. There's only like two hundred people."

"Maybe she *was* the wrong crowd."

"Someone had to help her get that illegal tattoo."

"Touché."

"So then she says, 'What is it you wanted to tell me?'"

"And you said . . ."

"I said, 'I just wanted you to know . . . I'm really looking forward to it, too.'"

"Déjà vu."

"Really?"

"Yep. Same story happened to me with Isabel. Well, except for the nose ring. She really had a nose ring?"

"Silver loop."

"And a tattoo?"

> **"Don't get me wrong. She's not dog ugly or anything."**

Lamar tapped the side of his left arm, right underneath his shoulder. "Right here. It's in Vivaldi font."

"Cool. I like that one."

On screen, Anakin was saying good-bye to his mother.

Lamar noted, "Don't get me wrong. She's not dog ugly or anything."

"Oh, no."

"I mean, she's no fancied-up Queen Amidala, but . . . I don't know . . . she's kind of a . . . Padmé."

"Hey, Padmé's better. Padmé's real. And, after all, Padmé is just a Queen Amidala in-the-hiding."

Lamar smiled. Silence, then, "Iz is kind of a Padmé, too, huh?"

Matt smiled, not taking his eyes off the TV screen. Lamar started chuckling. Matt started chuckling.

Matt's dad entered the room. He was chewing gum, wearing his usual jeans and a plaid shirt. "What are you guys laughing about?"

The boys stifled their laughs.

"Star Wars," Matt said truthfully.

Mrs. Calahan entered the room behind her husband. She was wiping her hands on a kitchen towel. "Hey, Lamar. You want to stay for dinner?"

"Definitely," Lamar said. "I'll let my mom know."

"Good," Mr. Calahan said. "I look forward to hearing the latest about a galaxy far, far away."

"You're home early, Dad," Matt said as he shoved a bite of peas into his mouth.

His dad nodded. "I've started working on refinishing the Zarza's basement across the street. It's nice working so close to home."

Matt's mom smiled.

"Speaking of which," Matt's dad said, "I saw Jacinto's daughter, Isabel, today."

"I like her so much," Matt's mom put in. "How is she?"

Matt's dad studied the ceiling, as if searching for the right word. Then he said, "Glowing."

His parents' heads snapped straight to Matt.

Matt dropped his fork onto his plate. "Okay, okay, fine, I asked her to the banquet."

His mom clapped. "Yea! She's safe."

"Safe?" Matt said.

"Yeah, no tattoos or anything."

Lamar buried his face in his hands.

"Actually, it's a disaster," Matt admitted. "Gill and Alfonzo split on us even though they gave us their word that they'd go with us."

"They must have a good reason," Mrs. Calahan submitted.

"I guess," Matt concurred. "Sure doesn't seem fair though."

"Well, hey," Mr. Calahan piped up. "How 'bout I drive you? Don't worry—I can be a *rad dad.*"

"No one says 'rad' anymore, Dad."

"Well, can I be . . . a . . . hoppin' pop?"

"Please don't."

"Can me and my date come with you, too?" Lamar asked.

"I thought this wasn't a date," Mrs. Calahan interrupted.

"It's not, it's a youth function," Matt and Lamar said at the same time.

"Sure, you guys can come," Matt's dad said to Lamar. "But won't your mom want to drive you?"

"No, she's going with a date herself," Lamar said. "It'd be too weird."

Matt's parents shared a gaze.

Lamar nudged Matt. "Hey!" he exclaimed. "Maybe your dad can help."

Matt's eyes grew wide. "Um, I don't . . ."

"Help with what?" Mr. Calahan asked.

Matt looked at his dad. *Well, he did understand plotting chapters . . .* "We're looking for pointers about what to do when we go to the banquet. How to act, that sort of thing."

Mr. Calahan broke into a wide smile and pushed his chair back. "Up! Up!" he shouted.

Matt and Lamar hesitantly stood up.

Matt's dad pushed them around the table and into the living room. He opened the front door and shoved them outside.

Then he closed the door in their faces.

Matt looked at Lamar. Lamar looked at Matt. Lamar shivered. "It's cold out here."

The door opened a crack, and Mr. Calahan tossed two jackets to the boys. He closed the door again.

Lamar gladly put on his jacket. "Did your dad just kick us out of the house?"

From behind the door, Mr. Calahan's muffled voice shouted, "No! Knock when you're ready to come in!"

Matt rolled his eyes, still holding his jacket in his hand. He knocked. As the door swung open, Mr. Calahan exclaimed, "Look who's here, Penny! It's Matt and his date!"

"What?" Matt and Lamar exclaimed in unison.

Then Lamar added, "I'm *his* date?"

Matt's mom's head popped up behind his dad's broad shoulders. "Play along," she coaxed. "You'll learn best by *doing*." Then she disappeared.

"Oh," Matt said. "Right. I get it." He turned to Lamar. "You're my date."

"Why do *I* have to be the girl?"

"Because it's my house. C'mon." Matt stepped into his foyer. His dad pushed him back out.

"Lesson one: Ladies first," he prompted.

"That's right!" Lamar agreed, pushing his way in front of Matt. "I can't believe you were just gonna leave me in the cold like that! Hmph!"

Matt shook his head. He entered behind Lamar. The boys stopped in the entryway and waited for instruction.

"Next, Matt, you help Lamar remove his coat. Then you take off your own."

"Mine's already off."

From the kitchen, Matt's mom said, "Matt ..."

"Okay, okay." Matt pulled at the jacket on Lamar's shoulders as Lamar turned around, nearly yanking his friend to the ground.

"Easy!" Lamar cried.

"Sorry."

"Man, Isabel's in for it."

"Shut up."

"Hey—that's no way to talk to a lady."

Matt rolled his eyes again. He handed both jackets to his dad, who put them away.

"This way." And Matt's dad led them to the kitchen. Matt made sure to let Lamar go first. When they arrived, Matt was shocked to see several more forks and plates on the table.

"What's this?" Matt asked. "It looks like Thanksgiving . . . but with macaroni and cheese."

"My kind of Thanksgiving," Lamar noted.

"All right," Mr. Calahan said. "Next, you have to seat Lamar." He walked to the other side of the table, where he pulled out his wife's chair. "Pull it out." He waved his hand toward the chair, palm out. "Allow her to sit." With a smile, Matt's mom sat down. "Then help her scoot in." He pushed the chair toward the table. "Now your turn."

Matt pulled the chair out. He waved toward it, and Lamar sat down. Matt pushed it in. Lamar gasped as his ribs crushed into the table's edge. "Owww!"

"Sorry."

Lamar pushed out and stood up. "Your turn. Let me practice."

Lamar pushed the chair back in and then pulled it out. He waved toward it. Matt sat down. Lamar jammed Matt into the table. "Owww!"

"Oh—so sorry." Lamar sat down beside Matt, who glared at his friend.

Finally Matt said, "Dad, are you sure about all this? I don't see people doing this stuff much any more."

Mr. Calahan nodded. "Well, times have changed, I suppose. Some girls may not want you to open their door or get their chairs. If they want to get it themselves, as a gentleman, let them. But more often than not, I think you'll find that girls like to be treated like princesses when they meet a prince."

Suddenly the cell phone rang. Matt's dad looked at the display. "Gotta get this. Be back in a sec." He flipped the phone open and left the room.

Matt's mom pointed to the place setting in front of her. "Okay, here's how eating works." There were two forks, the plate, then a knife and a spoon. At the top of the plate lay another fork and two small plates above it. "The first fork is for salad," she stated. "The one next to it is your meal fork. And the one above your plate is your dessert fork. Everything else is normal.

There are actually more settings than this, but I think this is good for now." She picked up her napkin. "Place your napkin on your lap and leave it there until you need it. When you want something somewhere on the table, ask for it politely. If someone else asks for something, pass to the right. Always to the right."

"This is getting confusing."

"I can make Cliffs Notes."

The boys dished out their meals and passed to the right, asking for butter or salt as needed. Mr. Calahan shortly returned and apologized for the interruption. As they ate, Matt's parents provided tips as they came to mind, including more than one "Take your time. Don't eat like pigs. Enjoy the moment."

"More than anything," Matt's dad offered, "be respectful and responsible. And honest. Just be real."

"Just be you," said Matt's mom with a wink.

Later that night, Matt, Lamar, Gill, and Alfonzo gathered in Matt's bedroom to look at the anonymous letter and website warning. The boys usually felt comfortable whenever they got together, but tonight Matt could feel a bit of tension in the room. Gill was nervous about his commercial. Alfonzo was still a little edgy about Matt taking Isabel to the banquet—and having another warning linked to the laptop didn't help. And, of course, Matt and Lamar were nervous about going to the banquet. The more the two of them talked about it, the more they felt jolted by Gill and Alfonzo. They were having to walk through forgiveness, which wasn't easy since there wasn't time. Matt knew they had to pull together *now*, because their common secret—the laptop—was commanding their attention.

Lamar studied the white index card Matt had received in the mail.

www.civd.org/messageformatt

"So what's on the website?" Lamar asked.

Matt let out a long breath, then typed the address into his browser. The simple white page popped up, exactly like the one Matt had seen when he first received the laptop. But, of course, this time the message was different. The boys leaned in and read:

> **This isn't a game. The Wordtronix is not a toy. Keep using it like a toy and they WILL find you. They don't stop. They don't let up. They don't tell the truth. If things seem bad now, you'll see—it can get much worse. Much, much worse.**
>
> **If I can, I'll contact you again in a more personal way. Remember, you have power in your hands. Be smart, or any day could be your last.**

Alfonzo shook his head and paced the floor. Lamar leaned back on Matt's bed. Gill sat on a couple of the milk crates. Matt slumped in his writing chair in front of the laptop.

"I don't like this," Alfonzo said. "This is dangerous."

Matt sat up straight. "Since when don't you like danger and adventure?"

Alfonzo stopped pacing. He didn't say anything, but he didn't have to. Matt *knew* when he stopped liking danger . . . when his sister was getting closer to being part of it.

"The question is: Who wrote this?" Lamar asked. "This looks exactly like the first warning you got, from Sam."

"But Sam's dead," Matt interjected. "Remember what that first warning said? 'If you've come here, then I must be dead . . .' I think this is someone else."

"Maybe it's from whoever killed Sam," Lamar suggested.

Matt shook his head. "I don't think so. This is from someone who's warning us . . . trying to help us. Maybe a friend of Sam?"

"Who cares?" Gill threw in for good measure. "All I know is that if this means we might have some killer in cowboy boots chasing us through the wilderness again, you can count me out."

"None of us want that," Lamar agreed. "But we can't just ignore this."

"What are we supposed to do about it?" Alfonzo offered. "What I don't like is that it could affect other people."

Here we go, Matt thought. He caught Alfonzo's eye. "Like who? Who knows about the laptop but us?"

"No one yet," Alfonzo said. "But whoever wrote this message is right. You keep using it, and others may find out."

"Like Isabel?" Matt pressed. "Alfonzo, I told you I don't want anyone else in on the secret. Don't worry."

Alfonzo's eyes narrowed. "It could be anyone, Matt. Iz, Hulk—your dad—who knows? Obviously whoever wrote this warning knows about it."

"Fine," Matt said. "Look: We need to vote. I say we stop using the laptop for a while—just till the heat dies down. And I'll just be sure no one else gets hold of it, as always. All in favor?"

Matt, Lamar, and Alfonzo all raised their right hand.

"No!" Gill cried. "No! Not three days before my commercial! You promised! You said I could trust you!"

"Gill, we've talked about this. You know there's no way I could have helped you anyway. I'll be at the banquet."

"That's right," Alfonzo put in. "With my sister."

"But you said I could trust you!"

"Actually, what I said is that I'd do my best." Then Matt added, "You'll just have to do this one on your own."

"But I'm gonna puke-a!"

Agitated, Matt jumped up. "Gill, did you read the message? Whoever wrote it said they want to contact me in a *more personal way*. You know what? I don't *want* them to contact me in *any* way. So if the only way I can protect myself is to let you toss your cookies on the ice, you'd better believe, you'll be upchucking to your heart's content!"

Gill's face was now red with anger. He stomped out of the room.

"Well, I think that's the best thing you've said all week," Alfonzo noted.

Lamar looked at Matt and raised his eyebrows.

"What?" Matt demanded.

Lamar shrugged.

Matt looked at Alfonzo, who was standing still.

"What?" Matt demanded again.

"You really gonna swear off the laptop?" he wondered.

Matt stared at the small, black computer sitting on his desk. "I'll do my best."

7

No Accident

Despite the cold, Matt was sweating again; this time it was his hands. As his father started the Toyota Camry—his mom's car—Matt crossed the street to the Zarza's. He felt uncomfortable, all dressed up in a sharp black suit and shiny black church shoes. The shoes were always so slippery. As he crossed into the Zarza's driveway, he straightened his tie—a forest green wonder his mom had discovered in his dad's closet. It was a nice addition, so long as he let his coat jacket cover up the tip, which sported a year-old barbeque stain.

Matt lightly touched the top of his head, and his hair prickled his palm. He knew he couldn't press down, or it would flatten the effect. He wished Lamar were there with him already. But he would be soon; they were picking up Lamar and Nicki on the way. He stepped onto the Zarzas' porch, then stood still for a moment. He glanced back over his shoulder and saw his dad reversing out of the garage. He could feel his stomach turning . . . churning.

The porch light was on, though it was only dusk. Matt remembered the first day he saw the Zarzas, when he used his laptop to blow out their porch light. Little did he know then, only a few months ago, what would be happening now. Who'd have guessed he'd be standing on the porch of the old house, butterflies in his stomach, eager to take Isabel to the 2:52 winter banquet? He closed his eyes and tried to relax.

He pressed the doorbell and heard a muffled *ding-dong!* Swallowing, he stood up straight, brushing the front of his coat. He heard footsteps drawing near. Suddenly the door opened. It was Alfonzo. It had been five days since they last met at Matt's house, and the tension between him and Alfonzo had dissipated quite a bit ... especially since Matt had sworn off the laptop. Gill, on the other hand, begged and pleaded every day for Matt to reconsider.

"¿Que pasa?"

"Hey," Matt said, feeling a little bit silly, but not sure why. Then, "Aren't you supposed to be at a hockey game?"

"Yeah, in a little bit. But I just wanted to make sure: you're not going to use the laptop on Isabel tonight, right?"

Matt nodded. "Really, you can trust me. My dad put me through a mini-Dale Carnegie course, so I wouldn't mess up."

"Better not."

"I won't."

"As long as I have your word."

"Just like I had your word about going to the banquet." It was a cheap shot, but it jumped out anyway.

"Look," Alfonzo said, lowering his voice, "let's forget about it, okay? Maybe I shouldn't have pulled out, but you know one of us had to be there for Gill."

"I know. He's pretty nervous."

"He ought to be. He has to eat a Pooka Dooka in front of the world, *and* he has to keep it down."

Matt nodded. "Hey, since I can't be there, you'll keep an eye on Hulk, right?"

"No problem."

Suddenly Isabel stepped into the foyer. Alfonzo moved aside as Matt gasped.

Isabel's brown eyes caught Matt's and then quickly looked down at the ground. Her midnight black hair was tied up in a bun, light wisps dancing on either side of her face. She wore a little bit of makeup—highlights on her eyes, cheeks, and lips— which he noticed because he'd never seen her wearing makeup before . . . and she wore it well. Her dress was a modest ensemble with long sleeves ending in ruffles. And it was forest green, matching Matt's tie perfectly. A shawl warmed her shoulders. Her shoes were black and shiny, probably with slick soles like his own. Matt smiled. *Queen Amidala in-the-hiding.*

"Your mouth is hanging open," Alfonzo said to Matt, loud enough for Isabel to hear.

Matt quickly snapped it shut and noticed Isabel smiling as she looked up at him and then down again.

Alfonzo slapped Matt on the chest. "See ya!" he said. Then he leaned in and whispered, "And if you mess up, you know I'll beat ya to a pulp." He winked and went inside.

Matt's attention shot to the left as he saw a curtain pull aside. He thought he saw Mr. Zarza for a second, but then he was gone. When Matt turned back, Isabel held out a small flower: a carnation dyed forest green. She handed it to him.

"Um . . . thanks," he said, not quite sure what to do with it.

She giggled. "Here." She took it back. "It's your boutonniere," she said as she pinned it on his jacket pocket. When she finished, she stepped back and looked at him.

"Thank you," Matt said again. And as the moment persisted, his eyes grew wide. *Was I supposed to get her a flower? To go with her green dress? Her forest green dress?* He couldn't believe it. They hadn't even made it off her doorstep, and he was already messing up. He felt his heart race. He opened his mouth to apologize when he felt a soft tap on his shoulder. He turned to see his dad standing there, a clear, plastic box in his hand. Inside was a forest green-dyed carnation.

"Here's your corsage for Isabel," his dad said with a wink.

"Heh-heh," Matt said as he took the box from his dad. It was cold. As his dad returned to the Camry, Matt popped the box open, thanking God for his parents. He removed the corsage, pulled the pin out of the back, and looked at Isabel. He moved forward slightly and then stepped back. He looked at her dress. "Um . . ."

Isabel giggled. "I'll put it on."

"Thank you," Matt said, relieved, and handed her the corsage.

A moment later, Matt opened the car door for Isabel. She slid inside, and after she pulled her dress in, he closed the door behind her. As he walked around the car, he just knew the night would be perfect. He took one last deep breath and opened his own door. As he slid inside, the sounds of his dad's "Rockin' 70s" CD filled the air. *Okay, so the evening would be* almost *perfect.*

Lamar entered the Camry looking sharp in a navy blue blazer and khaki pants. His tie was blue and gold. Since Isabel and Matt occupied the back, he opted for the front seat. He said hello to Mr. Calahan, Matt, and Isabel. When he saw Isabel, he glanced back at Matt quickly and then turned around. As

Matt's dad started driving again, Lamar tapped his leg to the beat of "We Are Family" by the Pointer Sisters.

Minutes later, after some shoddy directions from Lamar, Matt's dad pulled up to a small, brick house. Lamar thanked him and exited. Matt looked out the window to try to get the first look at Nicki, but his breath kept fogging up the glass.

At once, the car door by Isabel popped open, and Lamar helped Nicki into the backseat. Isabel scooted over beside Matt, which made him squeeze in closer to the door. He leaned forward and said "hi" to Nicki.

Nicki was a short girl with curly brown hair, clipped in the back. Sure enough, she had a nose ring— the first Matt ever saw up close. It was a small silver loop in the center of her nose. She wore dramatic makeup, though it seemed to fit her. Likewise, her blue, sleeveless dress wasn't quite as fancy as Isabel's but seemed to be just her style. Since she held her coat, Matt was able to catch a glimpse of her tattoo for a moment: NICKI. She leaned back and said something to Isabel that Matt didn't hear. Mr. Calahan played it cool. Matt wondered what his mom would have said if she were the driver tonight. Something like, "Oh, my goodness! What *is* that hanging out of your nose?"

> **Nicki was a short girl with curly brown hair. Sure enough, she had a nose ring.**

Matt peered back out the window. The car started rolling again as they headed to the banquet.

A mile later and the silence was deafening. Finally Matt's dad broke it. "So how's your mom?" he asked Lamar.

Lamar shrugged. "Good. She had to get there early."

"You know, I met your mom's new friend the other day. He seems nice."

"Hmm."

Matt's dad got out and opened the car door for the girls. On the driver's side, Nicki and Isabel exited, while Matt and Lamar exited from the passenger side. As he got out, Matt reached under his seat and pulled out his laptop, hoping his dad wouldn't notice. Lamar shot him a raised eyebrow. Matt and Lamar made their way around the rear bumper and met the girls. The crew waved good-bye to Matt's dad and headed toward the hotel entrance. They had almost disappeared into the hotel lobby when Mr. Calahan honked and caught Matt's attention. As his dad jumped out of the car, Matt stopped and told his friends to go on inside—he'd catch up in a second.

Matt clenched his laptop tight, ready to defend himself, when his dad caught him by surprise.

"Here." Mr. Calahan handed Matt his cell phone.

Matt looked at it for a long moment. "Dad, this is your cell phone."

Mr. Calahan laughed. "I know. I want you to have it tonight. So you can call me when the banquet is over."

"But what if you miss a business call?"

"I told you, Ace—I'm taking control of my business instead of letting my business control me. I've told my men, no business tonight. It's all yours."

Matt swallowed hard. "Okay, thanks." He clipped it to his belt and turned to leave.

"So," his dad quickly said, "are you sure you want to take your laptop with you?"

Matt looked down at the black, plastic laptop in his grasp. For a second, he considered giving it to his dad . . . but he knew he couldn't. Things had heated up too much, and Matt was concerned if anyone else had the laptop, he could be putting them in danger, too. Besides, Matt had learned that lately, danger had a habit of tracking him down . . . and he needed to be ready anytime, anywhere.

"Yeah," Matt said, "I need it . . . just in case."

Mr. Calahan narrowed his eyes. "Just in case *what?*"

This was the third time lately that Matt's dad had asked him directly about the laptop. "Inspiration."

Mr. Calahan twisted his lip. "Matt, you have to learn to let go."

"You don't understand," Matt said truthfully.

"I bet I understand more than you know," his dad said. Then he seemed to shrug it off. "Well, call me when you're ready to come home, okay?"

"K."

Matt and his dad parted ways.

Matt entered the hotel lobby, pushing through a revolving door. As he came out the other side, he met Lamar, Isabel, and Nicki, waiting patiently. They made their way to the banquet room, passing the check-in desk, a restaurant, a small waiting area with a TV, and a host of vending machines.

Up a flight of stairs, at the far end of a hallway that seemed to go on forever, they finally reached their destination. When they rounded the corner, they saw nearly thirty familiar faces from the youth group inside. The room was completely decorated now, the tables elegantly set. A white tablecloth covered each one, and a string of Christmas ivy lay over each table. Red and green candles flickered from inside glass jar centerpieces. A small, clear podium was at the front, and the boys' paper snowflakes dangled from the ceiling. Isabel was the first to step on the white paper walkway Matt had so meticulously measured. Matt motioned toward a vacant table, but Pastor Ruhlen headed them off at the pass. His hair was half red, half green, divided right down the middle.

"Howdy!" he exclaimed as if he were straight from the bloodline of Jesse James.

Matt smiled and gritted his teeth. *Please don't say anything about how we look!*

"Don't you look snazzy?" Ruhlen exclaimed. "And ladies, you are very beautiful tonight."

"Gracias," said Isabel.

Pastor Ruhlen offered his hand to Nicki. "I'm Pastor Ruhlen."

"Nicki," she said.

"Pleased to meet you. You're related to Hulk, aren't you? He mentioned you the other day." Pastor Ruhlen glanced at Lamar.

"Yeah, he's my cousin."

"Great. Well, hombres, have a seat. There's a table right over there. Dinner will be served in a few."

Matt and his friends made their trek to the table. On the way, Matt saw Lamar grimace at the sight of his mom and her date seated across the room. When they reached their table, Matt slipped his laptop under his chair. Next he pulled out a chair for Isabel. She didn't move. Then he realized she was still wearing her shawl. He scooted behind her and carefully helped her remove it, so as not to dislocate her shoulder. Not sure what to do with the shawl, Matt just hung it on the back of her chair. She didn't seem to mind. She moved in front of the chair and sat down. Matt helped push in the chair as she scooted forward. *So far, so good.* He carefully sat down beside her. Lamar and Nicki were now seated, too.

Matt looked at Isabel and smiled. She smiled back. Nicki looked at Lamar and smiled. He smiled back.

Lamar and Matt looked at each other and smiled.

"So . . . ," Matt said.

"So," Lamar said, "this is nice."

"I like the snowflakes," Isabel noted.

"I cut some of them out," Lamar boasted.

"They're nice," Nicki congratulated.

Matt looked at Isabel and nodded. She nodded back. Nicki looked at Lamar and nodded. He nodded back.

Lamar and Matt looked at each other and nodded.

"I wonder what's for dinner," Matt said, unfolding his napkin. He put it on his lap. Lamar, Isabel, and Nicki followed suit.

"I bet chicken," Lamar guessed.

"Chicken's always good," Nicki said.

Isabel noted, "In Mexico City, chicken is called *pollo*."

Nicki asked Isabel, "You've been to Mexico City?"

"I'm from Mexico City. I moved here in October."

"Your English is good."

"I grew up speaking both, but my Spanish is better."

Matt looked at Isabel and nodded and smiled. She nodded and smiled back.

Nicki looked at Lamar and nodded and smiled. He nodded and smiled back.

Lamar looked at Matt and nodded and smiled. Matt nodded and smiled back. He had to do something to get the conversation going. He said the first thing that came to mind.

"So," Matt said to Nicki, "what were you in for?"

"Huh?"

Crack! Matt jumped as Lamar's shoe smacked him in the shin.

Their conversation was (thankfully) interrupted when Lamar's mother stepped up. "Hello," she greeted. "How are all you elegant people tonight?"

The four friends muttered, "Fine" and "Good."

She addressed Nicki, holding out her hand. "I'm Lorraine Whitmore, Lamar's mama."

Nicki clasped her hand. "Nice to meet you. I'm Nicki."

Ms. Whitmore stepped aside. A handsome black man with graying hair nodded to the group. "This is Oscar," she introduced. Then she pointed around the table. "This is Matt and . . . Isabel, right? And Nicki. And you know Lamar."

Oscar nodded again. "Nice to meet you all. This is a nice banquet."

The four friends nodded their agreement.

"Well, we just wanted to stop by," Ms. Whitmore said with a wink. "You have fun tonight, baby dolls. I'm going to stay out of your hair, I promise." She gave a little laugh and then headed back across the room.

Lamar rolled his eyes.

"What?" Matt asked.

"I don't know," Lamar said.

"Are they dating?" Nicki asked.

Lamar nodded.

"They're cute."

"It's weird," Lamar said. "I'm at a winter banquet with my mother."

"He's a nice guy," Matt submitted.

"I guess. But he tries too hard to be funny."

"You should give him a chance. My parents might be right."

Lamar sat back and glared across the table at Matt.

Matt scratched his head. "In other words, Oscar may not be an Obi-Wan, but he's not a Darth Maul either."

Lamar's eyebrows went up. "So what is he then?"

"Kind of a . . . a . . ."

"Jar-Jar?" Isabel offered.

Matt threw his hand over his mouth as a burst of laughter erupted from the group.

"Yeah, that makes me feel a *lot* better!" Lamar said between laughs. "Thanks!"

At once, with the topic of *Star Wars* on the table, the conversation picked up. Matt explained why he liked Episode II better than Episode I. After a short prayer, the chicken came—Lamar was right about that—and Nicki shared her theory about Anakin's downfall. Matt was pleasantly surprised to find out Isabel knew a lot about the movies, too.

Halfway through dinner, Pastor Ruhlen stood up at the small, clear podium at the front. He tapped a glass with a butter knife and commanded the attention of the room. As the group continued their meal, he said, "I want to talk to you tonight for a moment—just a bitty bit—about something that hits us all during this season: Worry.

> **With the topic of *Star Wars* on the table, the conversation picked up.**

"Oh, yeah," Ruhlen said, his lanky form sliding around the podium. "There's lots to make you a worrywart during this time of year. Think about it. What are you worried about?"

Matt let out a sigh. *Let's see: Will Alfonzo beat me to a pulp for bringing the laptop? Will Gill hate me for not using the laptop? Will Hulk kill Gill just to get even? Would using the laptop at the hockey game really reveal our secret? Would Isabel explode if she knew I was thinking about the hockey game right now?* Matt looked at Isabel. She was intently listening to Pastor Ruhlen, soaking it up. A curly wisp of her hair danced around her ear.

Matt moved his foot and felt the hard plastic underneath his chair. He couldn't help it. He wasn't *trying* to think about Gill and the game and the commercial. But still . . . he hated not being there for his friend. *Then again,* Matt reminded himself, *Gill backed out first. It's his fault, not mine.*

"Yes," Pastor Ruhlen said, "there are a thousand things to worry about."

All of a sudden, a high-pitched, electronic whistling rendition of "Yankee Doodle Dandy" echoed throughout the room. Everyone looked at Matt.

"Perhaps," Pastor Ruhlen ad libbed, "you're worried your cell phone will ring at a most inopportune time."

Several kids laughed. Matt grabbed the phone on his hip, feeling his face flush rose red. Pastor Ruhlen stopped talking. Matt didn't recognize the number.

"Must be one of my dad's coworkers," he mumbled. He flipped the phone open and leaned into the wall.

Pastor Ruhlen continued speaking. "Anyway, as I was saying . . ."

"Hello?" Matt whispered into the phone.

"Matt?"

"Gill? How—how did you get this number?"

"Your dad. I told him it was an emergency."

"Gill!"

"What?"

"I'm kinda busy."

"Matt! I still can't keep a Pooka

Dooka down! I've tried all week, but

my mouth just spits it out! And Hulk is here, slapping his hand into his fist! He's going to do something—I'm sure of it! You have to use the laptop! You brought it with you, didn't you? I know you did, because you never let it out of your sight!"

You have to use the laptop!

"Gill, get hold of yourself," Matt said through gritted teeth. "I can't talk now. I'm busy." Matt hung up. Isabel, Lamar, and Nicki looked at him.

"Gill," he whispered.

Lamar's eyebrows popped up.

Matt turned to Isabel. "No big deal."

She looked at him for a long moment. "Are you sure?" she finally said.

"Yes, absolutely. Tonight is about us having a good time. Forget about it."

Isabel smiled, that twinkle in her eye. "Okay."

"So what do you do when worry hits?" Pastor Ruhlen asked. "As a 2:52 guy or girl, you should know. What you do is what Jesus said in John 14:1."

Pastor Ruhlen flipped open a Bible he produced out of nowhere. He read, "'Do not let your hearts be troubled. Trust in God; trust also in—'"

Yankee Doodle went to town a-riding on a pony!

Pastor Ruhlen stopped speaking again. Isabel smiled awkwardly at Lamar and Nicki. Matt excused himself, getting up this time. He grabbed the laptop from under his chair and exited the room.

Stuck a feather in his hat and called it macaroni!

Matt spun around the corner of the door and flipped the phone open. "What?"

"You said you'd help me! You're my friend!"

"Gill, this isn't the time for a guilt trip! We agreed to not use the laptop!"

"But this is an emergency! I'm going on the ice in just a little bit! I'm sick to my stomach! I thought you were going to do your best!"

"I am doing my best!" Matt shouted in a hush. "It's just—hold on." He unlatched the lid and hit the power button on the laptop.

"What are you doing?"

"Helping!" The laptop booted up, and Matt launched the word processor with a double click. He typed in:

```
Gill does fine.
```

Then he hit the clock key and shut down the computer.

"There."

"What there?"

"I fixed it. You'll do fine."

"What did you type?"

"I typed, 'Gill does fine.'"

"That's it?"

"Gill—I don't have time!"

"'Gill does fine!' Matt! You know how crazy your laptop works! You need to be specific! I need 'Gill remembers his lines!' I need 'Gill becomes an instant star!' I need 'Gill doesn't spew all over the ice!' 'Gill does fine' means nothing! It's too subjective! And what about Hulk?"

Gill was right, but Matt partly felt it served Gill right for reneging on the banquet.

"Gill, I have to go. You'll do fine. Trust me."

"Trust you?"

Matt slammed the cell phone shut. He took a deep breath, put the laptop away, and scooted back into the room. He quietly slid the laptop under his chair and switched the phone to "vibrate."

Isabel, Lamar, and Nicki stared at him.

"What?" Matt asked.

Isabel angled her head back and looked under the chair at Matt's laptop, a question mark on her face. Matt didn't say anything.

"You dropped some chicken on your tie," Lamar said, trying to change the focus.

Matt looked down. It was his dad's old barbeque stain. "Thanks for pointing that out, Lamar."

Isabel looked back at Pastor Ruhlen.

"So," the youth pastor finished, "it's important to remember we can trust God in *any* challenge. No matter how small . . . or how big. And just remember, sometimes it takes time."

That's easier said than done, Matt thought.

And then Pastor Ruhlen added, "Don't forget: As members of the 2:52 Youth Group, you know you can trust each other, too. You guys always amaze me how you're there for each other, pray for each other, and help each other—no matter what the cost . . ."

Matt heard no more. He stared at Pastor Ruhlen with his mouth gaping. He couldn't believe he had just said that. It was like rubbing salt in the wound. He knew from their set-up time that Matt and his friends were having their differences . . . and now . . . he was trying to make a point. Matt shook his head. Still . . .

Matt was so upset he could hardly focus. Upset at Pastor Ruhlen, upset at Gill. *What is Gill thinking? Calling during the banquet? Oh, sure, Gill wanted to know if he could trust me, but can I trust him?*

A few minutes of small talk among Lamar, Nicki, and Isabel passed, and Matt worked his hardest to relax. He knew he could recover from this embarrassment. He just had to focus.

A waiter came by with dessert. Matt felt his heart slowing down as the humiliation slithered away. Chocolate cake would help him focus. The waiter placed a large slice of fluffy cake down in front of Nicki, then Isabel, then Lamar, then just as he leaned in to set a serving down in front of Matt . . .

BZZZZZZZZZZZZZ!!!!!!

Matt jumped up with a scream as the phone vibrated like mad. His arm caught the waiter's arm, and his chocolate cake pitched into the air. As Matt tried to jump back, it flipped around like a wayward football, bits of dark frosting splattering like paint. Matt's leg caught on his chair as he knocked back into the waiter, and the cake was unforgiving. It slopped to a stop right in the middle of his chest. In pure reflex, Matt shouted, "Ugh!" and cast it away as if it were a poisonous spider . . . and it shot straight at Isabel. Her eyes grew wide as silver dollars as she lurched up and backward, but not far enough. The cake blotched onto her beautiful, forest green dress, right on her stomach. She screamed. Matt gasped. And the cake crumbled onto the floor.

> **Matt jumped up with a scream as the phone vibrated like mad.**

BZZZZZZZZZZZZ!!!!!!

The room fell quiet as Matt and Isabel stood there, egg on their faces, cake on their outfits.

BZZZZZZZZZZZZ!!!!!!

Matt grabbed the phone and flipped it open.

"Matt!" Gill cried. "I need help! I go on in less than ten minutes! I'm going to lose it!!"

"You're not the only one with problems," Matt snapped, and he smacked the phone shut.

Isabel stared at Matt for a long moment.

"I'm . . . I'm so sorry," Matt said.

"Was that Gill?" Isabel asked.

Matt barely nodded.

Her face hardened. "Why are you talking to Gill like that?"

Matt's eyes dropped to the phone in his hand.

"I'm going to clean up," Isabel muttered, and she marched out of the room.

Lamar and Nicki shared a glance and then looked back at Matt.

"I . . . I gotta clean up, too." Matt clipped the phone to his belt and walked out in a daze.

Halfway down the hall, he saw Isabel enter the women's bathroom.

"Isabel—"

The door shut behind her. He made his way to the men's bathroom, where he shuffled over to the sink and grabbed a paper towel. *Stupid, stupid, stupid!* After running the faucet for a moment, he wet down the paper towel with liquid soap and lukewarm water. He rubbed his shirt and tie where the cake had splattered, but it just made the stain spread.

"Perfect," he muttered. He put the paper under the faucet for more water, and the stream hit his hand—spitting droplets around the sink and on his pants. He jumped back. "Oh, GREAT!" he shouted. That's all he needed: to look like he wet his pants.

"Don't worry—it's only a stain."

Matt spun around, and his heart started pumping rapidly. The voice came from one of the stalls—the third one. The closed one. It sounded odd . . . like an electronic voice. Like it wasn't real, but distorted.

"Wh—what?"

"Worse things can happen. Believe me."

Matt gulped. "Wh-who's there?"

"A friend."

Matt leaned back and looked under the stall . . . but he didn't see shoes. He just saw boots. Thin cowboy boots.

Everything within Matt wanted to run in terror, but he was frozen, his back to the mirror and the sink. And his laptop was in the banquet room.

"You . . . you chased us in the wilderness . . . in Landes," Matt said boldly, referring to the boys' recent camping trip. "You sure don't seem like a friend."

The person behind the door chuckled. *"I wasn't chasing you. I was watching you. I had to know for sure that you had the laptop. That's why I wrote WORDTRONIX in the mud and in the window. I had to see how you would respond. I had to see if you knew what it meant. I knew one day you'd come . . . I just didn't know when."*

It made sense, but it still made Matt uncomfortable. "Who *are* you?" he asked.

"It's me, Matt. It's Sam."

8

Face-Off

Matt reeled. "What?"

"*It's Sam, Matt. The one whose cabin you blew up. Thanks a lot, by the way. Not that I cared much for the carpet. Wrong color.*"

Matt suddenly felt his head rushing. He spun around and shut off the running water. Then he whirled back around and stared at the closed stall door.

"But you're dead."

Sam sighed. "*So I've heard.*"

"But your message on the Internet said if we had the laptop, you must be dead. You're *not dead?*"

"*I wrote that because I thought if I ever lost the laptop, I would be dead. But I was wrong. Why do you think I hacked the website and wrote you another message? I had to let you know I was still alive.*"

"Why? Do you . . . want the laptop back?"

Another electronic chuckle. "*Heavens, no. You couldn't pay me to take the thing. Besides, as long as I don't have it, they can't find me.*"

"They?"

Sam ignored the question. *"As long as they think I'm dead, I can do more to stop them. And they must be stopped."*

"Who?"

"There's no time now. You'll find out soon enough, because I'm going to need your help. How much do you know about the laptop anyway, Matt? Do you know everything?"

Matt swallowed hard. "What do you mean? And how do you know my name?"

The boots under the door shifted. *"Matt, listen to me. Trust no one. No one. The moment you let your guard down, they will find you. They will deceive you, and they will find you."*

"I don't understand. Who? And what do you mean, do I know everything? Is there something else to know?"

"Trust no one, Matt."

"Is that it? Is that what you came to say?"

"Yes. When there's more to say, I'll find you."

Matt didn't like the sound of that. "But—"

"You see the changing table, Matt?"

Matt looked around the bathroom. Off to the side, by the stall closest to the wall, was a baby changing station. "Yeah."

"Go to it."

Matt cautiously moved over to it.

"Face it."

"Why?"

Sam's metallic voice ordered, *"Do it."*

Reluctantly, Matt did.

"Now, don't turn around."

Matt heard the stall door open and the shuffling of feet. His eyes shifted right, to the mirror over the sink, where he saw the back of Sam's figure exiting the bathroom. A long, black trench coat covered his body down to the top of his boots. An old-fashioned 1940s-style hat covered his head. He whisked out the door, his trench coat flowing behind him like a cape. As the door closed, Matt hesitated, then ran to the door and flung it open. But the long hall on the other side was empty. Sam had vanished.

Isabel stepped out of the women's restroom at the same time Matt stepped out of the men's.

"What's going on?" she asked.

Matt opened his mouth to speak.

"And don't say, 'nothing,'" she interrupted, "because I know something's up. You're acting strange. This whole evening is just . . . weird."

Matt looked up and down the hall again. Sam was nowhere around. He had literally disappeared. "I don't know what's going on," he muttered.

"Is this about missing the game? Or Gill's commercial? Would you rather be there?"

Matt's face snapped back to Isabel's. "Huh? No ... no. Absolutely not. I want to be here at the banquet more than anything. Honest."

"Then what? Is it me?"

Matt looked into Isabel's deep brown eyes. Her voice that normally sounded like newly spun honey sounded wounded. "Not at all," Matt said, reaching out toward her arm. "C'mon, let's go back in and enjoy our cake. I'm sorry. Let's just forget all this. It's over. I promise."

As they made their way down the hall, Matt asked Isabel if she got the stain out of her dress. She said it was hard to tell, but she'd be all right. Matt apologized again. He glanced back over his shoulder twice, to see if he might catch another glimpse of Sam, but he wasn't there.

But the long hall on the other side was empty. Sam had vanished.

When they reentered the banquet room and took their seats, Matt forgot to pull out Isabel's chair. But she didn't seem to notice.

"All better?" Lamar asked.

Matt nodded and gave him a look that said, "I don't want to talk about it." A new piece of chocolate cake sat at his and Isabel's spots. Matt practically forced himself to eat it. He just wasn't hungry.

Lamar talked about some comic books he enjoyed and which characters were the hardest to draw. Nicki seemed genuinely interested. Like Matt, Isabel didn't say much. She just worked her way through her cake.

Matt's ears began to ring. He tried to block it out, but all he could hear were Sam's words echoing in his mind, in that metallic, electronic voice: *"Trust no one. No one. Trust no one, Matt."*

Matt glanced down at his cell phone. In his mind, he heard Isabel asking, "Why are you talking to Gill like that?"

Matt closed his eyes.

"I thought I could trust you!" he heard Gill shout.

"Trust me," he heard himself plead with Alfonzo, with Gill, with his mom.

"It's not just a matter of trust," his mom's voice echoed. "It's a matter of responsibility, too."

"Trust no one," Sam warned, hiding behind a door, behind a mask, behind a false voice.

He heard Pastor Ruhlen again. "You guys always amaze me how you're there for each other, pray for each other, and help each other—no matter the cost."

Then Matt saw a flash before his eyes—Alfonzo pushing him, and Matt insisting, *"Trust.* That's what the four of us—the QoolQuad—are all about, right?"

Matt put down his fork. He placed his hand on the phone by his side. Any minute, Gill would be sliding out on the ice, delivering his commercial. He was facing one of the biggest challenges of his life . . . and Matt wasn't there for him. He told Gill he could trust him . . . but he wasn't being trustworthy. He wasn't being the QoolQuad friend he needed to be. He wasn't being that 2:52 example of integrity, honesty . . . and trust. Matt felt his palms begin to sweat. Sam was wrong. Matt *could* trust someone. Matt could trust Lamar, Gill, and Alfonzo. Matt could trust his best friends. But if he chose to take Sam's advice and live in fear, he could lose his friends. He could lose the QoolQuad—those he trusted most.

"Matt?"

Matt looked up.

"Matt, are you all right?" Isabel asked. "I've said your name three times. What's going on?"

Matt pushed his chair back. "I've got to go." He yanked the laptop out from underneath his seat and jumped up from the table. As he hurried off, he heard Lamar say, "He probably just dropped more cake on his tie. He loves that tie."

As Matt marched down the hall, he popped open the laptop and hit the power button. He reached the stairs and took them two by two as the Wordtronix logo spun around on the screen. He took a quick left, then made his way to the small waiting room, off from the lobby, where he had seen a television set.

He hurdled a sofa in the center of the room and sank into the cushion. He snatched the remote off an end table and flipped the TV to channel 4, then tossed the remote onto the cushion next to him.

On screen, announcers who sounded like Abbott and Costello were recounting the last play. Then Abbott said, "Well, before we go to a commercial, we have this word from Pooka Dookas."

Costello jumped in with, "Pooka Dookas are supa-dupa!"

"Yes, they certainly are."

Matt opened the word processor and let his fingers hover over the home row of his keyboard. "Get ready to do just fine, Gill," Matt whispered. "Really. You can trust me."

On the television, the camera shot pulled back to show the entire hockey rink, and . . . there was Gill! On TV! He stood at the far side of the rink, in the crazy white and purple polka-dot suit he had worn during his practice. Matt squinted and thought he could see first, Alfonzo, and then, Hulk's unmistakable figure behind him. At once, polka music filled the arena, blasting from loudspeakers.

Boo-buhda-boo-boo! Boo-buhda-boo-boo!

As the crowd booed and hissed, Matt quickly typed:

```
The hockey crowd, while rowdy, started
to enjoy the polka music. It was like a
Gill-fan-polka-fest!
```

Matt hit the key with the clock face on it. Immediately the laptop's on-screen cursor turned to a small clock that ticked forward fast as lightning. Suddenly from the television came an uproar of boos and hisses that quickly faded into stomps bursting from around the arena.

Boo-buhda-boo-boo! Boo-buhda-boo-boo!

Matt smiled wide. They were stomping to the beat of the polka music!

Boo-buhda-boo-boo! Boo-buhda-boo-boo!

Full of energy, Gill slid onto the ice, a colorful bag of Pooka Dookas in his hand. The crowd cheered as he strutted forward like a chicken, like only Gill on ice could. Men shouted heartily, and woman screamed with laughter.

The camera closed in on Gill's face—staring right at Matt through the large TV screen. He was a natural. His pearly whites and red hair gave him the appearance of a born clown, but without the need for makeup.

Gill paused as the music softened and the arena calmed. Matt added:

> With the speed of a computer, Gill
> remembered his lines perfectly and
> delivered them flawlessly. He was a
> force to reckon with! He was Gill-da-man!

At once, Gill exclaimed, "Kids! Looking for something sweet and crunchy? Pooka Dookas!"

He did a little jig. Cheers erupted.

He pulled a Pooka Dooka out of the bag. "Parents! Looking for something with a nutritious surprise inside? Pooka Dookas!"

More cheers. More dancing.

"Looking for something that will put a spring in your step? A jolt in your jog? A kick in your dance?"

"You bet I am!" Matt said aloud.

"Then get Pooka Dookas—now in three new colors, including polka dots! Just one taste and you'll say"—Gill was about to reach into the bag and pull out a Pooka Dooka, when he was suddenly distracted. His eyes flashed to the side.

"What? What?" Matt cried. "Eat one! Say 'Pooka Dookas are supa-dupa!'"

The camera angle suddenly switched, and another camera focused on someone entering the rink ... someone who wasn't wearing skates. Matt leaned forward. *Oh, no.* The "someone" was big. The "someone" was strong. The "someone" obviously had revenge on his mind. It was Hulk Hooligan.

Matt's fingers flew to his keyboard, but he didn't make it in time. Hulk smashed into Gill like a wrecking ball into a brick wall. Gill slammed onto the ice, and the bag of Pooka Dookas flew out of his hand, scattering cookies across the rink. The crowd roared.

"Was that supposed to happen?" Abbott asked.

Matt could hear Costello shuffling papers. "I don't think so. What's going on?"

Matt felt the heat rising in his body. Hulk wasn't going to ruin this if he could help it. "Well, Alfonzo," Matt said, "it's time for you to skate with the big boys."

> Alfonzo, sports guy extraordinaire, remembered what Hot Shot Howard taught him. In moments, he had a pair of skates on his feet, and he was on the ice.

Foooooooom! Like lightning, Alfonzo shot onto the rink, speed skating straight ahead, hockey stick in hand.

"Maybe this *is* part of the show," Abbott said.

"I think it is indeed," Costello answered.

"He needs help," Matt whispered.

> One by one, the HockPucks entered the ice. They were about to play a new kind of hockey.

One! Two! Three! Four! Five! The HockPucks slid into the arena taking their places around the ring. As Gill regained his stance, Alfonzo sped around him. Hulk shouted at Alfonzo and tried to block him. Alfonzo maneuvered around Hulk and slid straight toward the scattered cookies.

Smack! Smack! Crack! Crack! Alfonzo smacked one cookie after another with his stick, sending them to player number 63. Number 63 passed them to number 56. Number 56 passed them to 94 and so on, around the rink.

Matt typed,

> Hot Shot Howard is the last to get a pass.

As the Pooka Dookas made their way through the formation, Hulk headed back toward Gill. Gill scooted away from Hulk's advance, toward his starting spot.

"Polka boy!" shouted Hot Shot Howard.

Gill's head snapped forward. Howard smacked a Pooka Dooka, and *wham!* it shot forward—straight into Gill's mouth! The crowd went wild! Matt jumped up and punched the air. "Yes! Yes! Yes!"

Wham! Wham! Wham! Three more right into Gill's open mouth with a precision that only Hot Shot Howard could have provided.

The polka music fired up again, and the crowd jumped to their feet and started dancing. The hockey players bypassed Hulk and speed skated to Gill, lifting him up on their shoulders.

"POOKA DOOKA!" the players shouted.

"POOKA DOOKA!" the crowd shouted.

"POOKA DOOKA!" Matt shouted.

Even Carl the ad manager was jumping up and down. The camera pushed in toward Gill, who was chewing happily. Hulk stood off to the side, looking frustrated and upset. Gill looked straight at the camera and, after victoriously swallowing, he exclaimed, "Pooka Dookas are supa—"

And he hiccupped.

"Are supa—"

And he put his hand on his chest.

"Are . . ."

The cheers slowly died down as the crowd fixed their attention on Gill. As he looked more and more uncomfortable, the camera pulled back, and Matt saw Hulk flexing his muscles and laughing. If Gill couldn't get through this, Hulk would still have had his revenge . . .

Abbott asked, "Is he all right?"

"I think he's turning green."

Gill *was* turning green. Matt quickly sat down and typed in the laptop:

```
Gill's stomach settled d█
```

That's all the further Matt got before Hulk shoved his way in front of Gill to proclaim his victory. Gill, bless his heart, leaned forward over Hulk and, in front of the entire arena, and in front of the nation, he—

BZZZT!

Matt blinked. The TV turned black. His gaze moved to the cushion beside him. The remote was gone. Matt quickly snapped the laptop shut and slowly turned around.

There stood Isabel, the remote in her hand, glaring at Matt.

The Good, the Bad, and the Ugly

9

Isabel shot out a sentence in Spanish.

"Huh?" Matt said. Then, "Wait, let me explain."

Isabel folded her arms across her chest, her deep brown eyes glassy and her lips tight.

"Please don't be upset. I know it hasn't been the perfect night, but it's just . . . well . . . I had to . . . um . . ." Matt blinked. ". . . um . . ." He couldn't figure out how to say it without revealing any secrets and possibly putting her in danger. "Well, okay, I can't really explain, but . . ."

"I should have known," Isabel said softly, her eyes piercing Matt.

Matt's forehead wrinkled. "What's that supposed to mean?"

Isabel tossed Matt the remote control. "It means I'm ready to go home. You can call your dad." She spun around and walked away.

"Where are you going?" Matt called after her.

"To get my wrap."

Matt tried to think of something more to say, something clever, but his mind was blank. Isabel disappeared, and after feeling so elated, Matt felt stung, hurt, and completely confused. Numb from head to toe, he crumpled onto the sofa.

A few moments later, Lamar and Nicki passed through the lobby and doubled back when they spied Matt in the waiting room. Lamar walked up to the sofa. "Hey, is everything all right? Where'd you go? We just passed Isabel."

"Everything's fine." Matt yanked his dad's cell phone off his belt and dialed home.

"Hey," Lamar said, "Nicki and I are going to ride home with my mom and Oscar."

Matt looked up, surprised. "Really?"

"Yeah. He may be a Jar-Jar, but, you know, the more you watch Jar-Jar, the less he irritates you."

Matt nodded. "I know what you mean."

Lamar nodded back with a smile.

Matt's dad answered the phone. Lamar waved himself away as Matt asked his dad to return to the hotel.

"I'll be there in a few minutes," his dad assured him. "So how did your evening go, Ace?"

"Peachy, just peachy."

The ride home was silent and tense ... save the repeating chords of B. J. Thomas's "Raindrops Keep Fallin' on My Head." The song became even more appropriate when it began sprinkling outside. Matt's dad kept peeking into his rearview mirror, looking at Isabel, then at Matt, as if to ask, "What in the world happened?"

When they *finally* arrived home, Matt exited the vehicle. He grabbed a foldaway umbrella from the backseat pocket and unfolded it. He was about to walk over to open Isabel's door, when she opened it herself and stepped out. He scurried to her side, to try to keep her dry. She shut the door, ignoring him.

I'm sorry about the cake.

With speed, she shot by him, though he struggled to keep up. "You're going to get wet!" he exclaimed.

"Maybe it'll wash the chocolate out of my dress." She continued walking. Matt kept up with her.

"I'm sorry," Matt said. "It's just hard to explain."

"I don't *need* an explanation," Isabel retorted.

"Really—I'm sorry about the cake."

Isabel stopped. "The cake? The cake? You actually think I'm upset because of chocolate cake?"

"Well, chocolate cake on your dress and—"

"And you running out of the room and answering phones and playing on your computer and watching TV and making excuses and"—Isabel spouted off the rest of the sentence in Spanish. Matt didn't want to know the translation.

"W-well," he stammered, "how can I make it up to you?"

Isabel stepped back and let the cold, sprinkling rain hit her face like a thousand teardrops. She placed her hands on her hips and stared at him through tight eyes. Softly hoarse, she said, "You told me when they announced the banquet, I was the first one you thought about."

He nodded. "It's true."

"Next time, think harder." Isabel spun on her heel and escaped to her porch.

Matt tried to think of just one more thing to say, but nothing sounded quite right. He found himself loathing his laptop and the secret it made him keep. Matt let his umbrella drop, and the cold rain chilled him as Isabel slammed her front door shut.

Matt told his parents he didn't want to talk about the banquet tonight ... because he didn't really know what to say. They understood and said they were there for him whenever he was ready. Now, he sat in his bedroom chair sulking, twirling his boutonniere.

Suddenly a rap came at Matt's bedroom window. Surprised, he jumped up from his seat and fell over backward. As his heart calmed, he stood up and opened the window for Gill, who jumped out of the tree and rolled into Matt's bedroom. It had stopped raining, but his shoes were wet.

At once, Gill stood up and drew all Matt's curtains, peering between the cracks at the street.

"What are you doing?" Matt demanded.

"You can't be too careful," Gill replied.

"Of what?"

"Hulk. He's after me. He's going to kill me."

Matt nodded and sat down on his bed. "Well, at least he's off my back for once."

When he was convinced the coast was clear, Gill spun around and smiled wide. "This has been a *great* night." He pushed the air in front of him with his hands as he spoke.

"Really?"

"Really. Thank you *so much.*"

"What makes you think I had anything to do with it?" Matt gazed at the closed laptop on his desk.

"Oh, pah-leeez!" Gill shouted. "Pooka Dookas shot around the rink and then land- ing in my mouth? That totally has the signature of your amazing writing genius."

Matt's mouth upturned slightly. "Well, I can't take all the credit. Hot Shot Howard *is* a great shot. And we'll have to thank Alfonzo for being ready."

"Let's put the video on our web page when you finish it. That was soooo cool."

"I'm glad it worked out. You're famous, Gill. A famous redhead."

"I know I'm famous because I already have a stalker after me. A *big* one. Did you see me? I hurled all over Hulk in front of the world. It was classic! But, of course, I'm a dead man."

"But of course. The price of success."

"Aye. So how'd your big date go?"

Matt shrugged. "It was really just a youth function. Believe me." Gill didn't take his eyes off Matt. He continued, "Let's just say that was probably the *last* youth function I'll ever go to with Isabel."

"That bad?" Gill shrugged this time. "Oh, well. That's what your laptop's for. Just fix it."

Matt waved the idea away. "No way. I've about had enough of that thing for one evening. Besides, I gave Alfonzo my word." Matt considered telling Gill about his encounter with Sam but then decided to wait until the whole QoolQuad was together.

Gill nodded. "Well, just wanted to say thanks. You're a great friend. When I'm rich and famous, I'll remember you."

"Thanks."

A few minutes later and Matt was alone again. He closed his bedroom door and knelt beside his bed. He didn't close his eyes, but he stared at the forest green boutonniere in his hand.

"God, I know I did the right thing by helping Gill out tonight," he admitted. "But everything got so crazy, I ruined my evening with Isabel. And for her sake, I can't tell her why. I guess you know what's going on, and you know how to fix it. So I put it in your hands. I'm going to trust you. Please give me an answer. Help me sort through all this garbage and—" Matt stopped praying. He squeezed his eyes tight. It was Friday night . . . and he still had to take out the trash. "I just give it to you. In Jesus' name."

Matt pushed himself up and trekked downstairs. As he passed by the living room, he saw his mom and dad watching TV. He entered the garage and hit the door opener. Once the door was up, he dragged the trashcan down the driveway. As he walked, the bottom rim of the can ground against the concrete like fingers on a chalkboard. At the corner, Matt opened the can and threw his flower on the top of the trash bag inside, then closed the lid.

"Hola."

Matt spun around and looked over at the Zarzas' house. Alfonzo stood by the mailbox. Matt's eyebrows shot up. The Spanish boy nodded toward Matt and slowly crossed the street.

"Hola," Matt returned, not sure what else to say.

power play

Alfonzo twisted and sat on the edge of Matt's trashcan.

"Gill was just over," Matt said. "You guys just got back, huh?"

"Yeah."

It was dark, except for a few dim lights here and there. Matt looked at the streetlight reflecting on the wet street. He decided not to mince words.

"Hey, uh, I know you know I brought the laptop with me. But I promise: I never used it on Isabel."

"I know."

"You do?"

"She's pretty upset. I figured if you used it on her, *she'd* be here right now instead of me."

Matt nodded. He noticed a glow in an upper-story window of the Zarza's house—Isabel's bedroom. She was still up.

"So obviously, I totally messed up our banquet. You want to beat me to a pulp now or later?" Matt asked, bracing himself.

Alfonzo let out a sigh. "Neither."

Matt leaned back on the trashcan beside Alfonzo. "Really?"

"You did the best you could," Alfonzo reasoned. "The truth is, you and Lamar shouldn't have had to go to the banquet alone. I should have been there for you, too. Just like you were there for Gill." Then, "Besides, I can't beat you up. I'm too tired."

Matt smiled. After a moment, he admitted, "Still, you don't know how much I want to just push a button and fix everything."

"But you won't. Because you gave me your word."

"How come I can use the laptop to help Gill and help Gill's dad and help Hulk's brother and help Hulk ... but when it comes to helping me, I feel guilty?"

Alfonzo looked up at the streetlight and shrugged. "I think it's because you're a decent guy, Matt. That's why you got the laptop instead of me, or Lamar or Gill. We'd go loco with it. But you ... you think things through. You're the smart one, remember?"

> I feel like this laptop is starting to control my life.

Matt chuckled. "I was thinking just the opposite. I feel like this laptop is starting to control my life. Like my dad, with his phone. That thing controlled his life for years. He's finally got it under control, I think, but it wasn't easy."

"Maybe it just takes time," Alfonzo encouraged.

"I don't know. I think I'm about to lose my grip on everything," Matt admitted. "And meanwhile, I do stupid stuff like ruin your sister's evening."

Alfonzo nodded. "Well, maybe you should let your dad in on our secret. Maybe he can help."

Matt looked at Alfonzo. "Really? You think I should?"

"Well, you've got to do something, because Iz needs someone like you in her life right now."

Matt about dropped his jaw. "You'd trust me with her again?"

Alfonzo placed a hand on Matt's shoulder. "You're about the only one."

Matt smiled.

A few moments later, Alfonzo stood up and walked back to his house.

Matt looked up at the Zarzas' house. Isabel's silhouette filled her window, and she looked down at Matt. Matt lifted his hand and waved sheepishly. Her figure disappeared, and the room went black. He wondered how long she'd been watching . . . and if she heard the conversation.

How Matt wished he could explain everything to Isabel . . . explain why he was acting so crazy . . . explain the truth . . . but he *had* to protect her. He couldn't put her in danger for *anything*. Especially for himself. Besides, he reasoned, if she knew his heart . . . if she would ever know his heart . . . she would see through the layers of complexity. She would see. He knew he just had to trust God.

Matt looked up at the dark, cloudy sky again. Lamar had said that if they messed up, they might regret their very existence. But Matt didn't. After all, the evening wasn't a total disappointment. He did get to sit next to Isabel between the craziness . . . and talk about *Star Wars* . . . and he wouldn't trade anything for hearing the sound of her giggle when he attempted to pin on her corsage.

Matt stood up straight and lifted the lid off the trashcan. He pulled out the little forest green flower.

Matt was convinced. This was only the beginning. He'd heard that sometimes trusting God took time. And if he was truly going to trust God to help him, he wasn't about to give up now. He recalled his prayer and surmised that life isn't just a book. It's a whole series of books. And you can bet, there is a sequel on the way.

Epilogue

The following morning, Matt awoke to a sudden rapping at his window. His heart racing, he jumped out of bed and tripped over his desk chair. This was it. Either Sam had come to get him or Alfonzo had come to his senses and was going to beat him up for what he did to Isabel. He slowly peeked around the corner of his bed to see who it was.

It was Gill. Again.

Matt hopped up and quickly opened the window. Gill jumped in.

"Matt, you've got to help!"

"Hulk's not going to kill you," Matt assured his friend, not so convincingly.

"It's not Hulk I'm worried about! It's my mom! She just went into labor!"

"What?"

"Yeah, I'm gonna be a bother! Er—brother! Maybe both!"

"That's great!"

Gill ran over and snatched up the laptop. He threw it into Matt's hands. "You have to come now!"

"What am I going to do?"

"I've never seen my mom like this! She's crazy! I need you to ride with us and type and make sure she gets to the hospital safely!"

"Well, I . . . I'm still in my pajamas."

"Nice SpongeBob PJs, by the way."

"Thank you."

"C'mon! Change! Fast! You have to help! I can trust you, right?"

Matt smiled. "Give me a minute."

To be continued . . .

The 2:52 Boys Bible, NIV

General Editor, Rick Osborne

Helping boys ages 8 to 12 become more like Jesus mentally, physically, spiritually, and socially—Smarter, Stronger, Deeper, and Cooler!

Hardcover 0-310-70320-4
Softcover 0-310-70552-5

Laptop 3: Explosive Secrets

Written by Christopher P. N. Maselli

Softcover 0-310-70340-9

Techno thrillers that will keep you on the edge of your seat—2:52 Soul Gear™ Laptop series!

Bible Heroes & Bad Guys

Written by Rick Osborne

Softcover 0-310-70322-0

Comic book action straight from the pages of the Bible—2:52 Soul Gear™ non-fiction books!